THE RECKONING

Published by Snowy Wings Publishing.
snowywingspublishing.com

ISBN: 978-1-946202-35-2

Interior formatting by Key of Heart Designs.
Interior graphics by Vectorian.
Cover design © 2017 by Lia Wayward.
Photo copyright: leolintang / 123RF Stock Photo.

This book is dedicated to my husband, Mark, who has supported me
through all my times of reckoning.

The Reckoning

The Forest Spirit Series, Book Three

T. Damon

Chapter 1

Two cloaked, hooded figures slid into a small opening on the southernmost side of Lapis Mountain, and entered a cave that had not seen the light of a torch since long before the falling in the Forest. The figures, though crouched, were much larger than a nymph, and substantially bigger than a troll. They resembled humans, but weren't susceptible to most of the unfortunate aspects of being a human that frequently plagued the common non-magical folk. They were, in fact, warlocks—but far more powerful than one's standard, every day magical warlocks. These two happened to be brothers—and half of the coven of the Controllers.

"He will come," one Controller rasped, glancing for a moment at the crescent moon tattooed on his wrist. "He will want to know why we are here."

"He may have ignored our message," said the other.

"Trust me, Elec," he said, setting the torch on a stone protrusion that ran the length of the cave. Something within the bottom groove of the stone burst into flames and roared down the shelf, lighting up the entire room. He turned to his brother and said, "Magus will come."

His brother sighed loudly.

"Nobody invited *me* to the party!"

The Controllers lowered the hoods of their cloaks and looked up at the shrill voice that had penetrated their ears. Someone had indeed arrived, but it wasn't who they expected.

The Controller called Elec groaned in exasperation. "Nice for you to arrive, Bellis."

"So nice of you to include me, Elecampane," the woman snapped. She nodded at the other. "Mullein." A smile cracked her lips.

"Bellis." Mullein returned her smile with a sly grin.

"What do you want, Sister?" Elecampane asked with a grumble. "Too much pollution in the ocean, so you had to come here to annoy us?"

"I am not annoyed by her presence," Mullein said. "She has as much a right to be here as we do. We were going to need to send for her soon, anyway."

Elecampane snorted, and seemed to somehow float while his feet still remained on the ground. He'd always had that airiness about him, with his pale, almost translucent complexion, his ghost-white wisps for hair and deep gray eyes. His flighty personality was another story.

"He's right," Bellis said. "The same immortal blood that runs through your veins graces mine. Now what are you two up to in here? My moon has been burning for days."

"None of your business," Elecampane sneered. "Leave us alone, we're not done yet. We were going to send a reebob for you and Celandine when your presence is required."

"Okay, baby brother. I'll leave as soon as I get the answers I seek."

Bellis's cerulean eyes scanned the cave, using her long eyelashes to sweep away the ash that leaped forcefully from the bonfire. Though her eyes were not apt to change color upon will, her iridescent hair seemed to continually shift from a deep indigo to a sea-foam green, and all the colors of the spectrum in-between. She had a slender body, and walked a bit duck-footed, which was awkward on land, but highly effective when swimming in the ocean, which was where Bellis preferred to spend most of her time. She briefly caught the eye of her older brother Mullein, who was standing near the entrance to the cave, keeping watch but occasionally glancing back at his favorite little sister. His features were fairly rugged and effortlessly masculine, and he was as wide as he was muscular. He kept a beard to the length of his Adam's apple, which was a deep chestnut brown to offset his striking green eyes. The whole family was terribly attractive, no doubt, but why wouldn't they be? They were the Controllers: an ancient ageless, coven of siblings that had been cast from the Forest by the Higher Spirits long ago.

Bellis grinned when she noticed her brother's Book of Shadows resting on a carved oak table, and snatched it up, rifling through the loose pages.

"Give me that!" Elecampane cried. In one swift motion, he twisted himself into a spinning tornado and soared across the cave, lifting up his sister in an angry, swirling smoke. Bellis simply flicked her wrist, and water replaced the air, spiraling into a tidal wave and crashing to the ground, taking the two Controllers with it. They slid across the floor, skidding to a halt right at Mullein's feet.

"This is exactly why we were cast out of this Forest in the first place!" Elecampane shouted, grabbing his book and holding it tightly to his chest. "You have no discretion!"

"Brother, it is *you* who has no discretion," Mullein replied, holding back a deep, bellowing chuckle that was trying to escape his throat. "And

Bellis, if you must know, we are doing exactly what we *said* we'd do back when we were first cast out, separated from each other in our elemental realms. But it has been too long, my brother and sister. The time has finally come."

"Is that why my moon burns?" Bellis asked, holding out her left wrist. Mullein did the same, as did finally Elecampane. All three tattoos were enlarged in size and seemed to move on their own, as if waxing and waning in a distant twilight mist.

"Yes. The barrier enacted to keep us out must have faded. I knew it would, eventually." He paused for a moment. "Of course, we couldn't have done it without the help of Gorgon and our little friends, so we musn't forget their part in it."

"And what does that mean?"

"It means, my sister, that the Higher Spirits have been compromised. The Forest is so out of balance that all barriers have weakened, or faded completely. We can enter again! We can reclaim what was rightfully ours!"

"So that's why I was able to enter the vortex. And I wondered about all the reebobs. They were attacking everyone else but they just let me pass through. Hmm."

Elecampane sighed loudly before opening his mouth to speak to his sister. "When you're done being as intelligible as the sea stars you use as a pathetic excuse for a tunic, we can..."

"Ahh. I see what's going on here."

The three siblings whirled around. "Magus," they whispered in unison.

"And the Controllers," Magus replied, as if the mere sight of the three made him both exasperated and uneasy at the same time. "Though minus one, I see."

"She's on her way," Elecampane said. "Obviously you received our message, wizard."

"How could I not? Delivered by possessed reebob! You are all still just as dramatic as ever."

"And you, weak as ever," Mullein broke in. "But we already knew that."

Magus chuckled. "Well, while I must admit it has been lovely catching up and receiving the endless supply of compliments your family is famous for, if you requested my presence just to berate me, I really must go. Reebobs are possessed and running wild, and vortices are opened that should not be opened. Oh! But you already knew that, too." He turned and began to leave.

"Wait," Mullein said. "You care not for the fate of your precious Forest?"

"Now, this topic interests me." Magus turned back around. "What is it exactly that you are doing? Destroying the Forest? Because that's been attempted before, and it has failed. Numerous times, in fact. So I suggest you hop on whatever brooms you flew in here on and scram, because this Forest doesn't want you. You weren't wanted then, and you're not wanted now."

"I beg to differ," Elecampane said. "I think this Forest could use a little sprucing up. I think the Under Spirits would agree with us, too."

"The Higher Spirits won't."

"The Higher Spirits are outnumbered," Mullein said. "As are the beings of light. We've been gone a long time, indeed, but that hasn't stopped some of our most loyal supporters from visiting."

"Who, Gorgon?"

"Yes, and the other Under Spirits. But there have been more," Elecampane hissed. "So many more."

"Some beings of light aren't shining so bright anymore," Bellis chimed in. "Even I have gotten visitors from very influential kingdoms…"

"Why did you want me here, then?" Magus asked, not intending for his voice to sound as shaky as it did.

"We need leverage," Elecampane replied. "Something to ensure that we can't be touched again."

"What does that have to do with me?"

"Everything," Mullein said as he and his brother encircled the wizard. A strong gust of wind blew Magus farther into the cave, where Bellis trapped him in a sphere of water suspended above the ground. The old wizard lifted his arms forcefully and tried to speak an incantation, but Elecampane quickly made a zipping motion with his thumb and forefinger, and a burst of air knocked Magus off his feet, sending him sinking to the bottom of the water. He bobbed around for a moment, trying to regain his footing, but his limbs had grown weak in his old age and his magic was no use against three very powerful warlocks.

"Give him an air bubble, so he can breathe but not speak," Bellis ordered. Elecampane rolled his eyes, annoyed at the forcefulness of his sister's request, but obliged. Magus looked on helplessly, blinking frantically but unable to do anything to help his situation.

"We know the best warriors will come looking for your assistance. That will be just the distraction we need to put forth our real plan," Mullein explained. "Drop him, my sister."

Bellis released the wizard, who fell to the ground with a thud. Mullein wasted no time thrusting his fist into the wall and cracking four long, jagged stalactites around the wizard's body, with four smaller ones wrapping around his arms and legs, pinning them to the floor.

Mullein paced back and forth in front of Magus, stroking his beard as if pondering something. After a few moments, he stopped, holding out his large, calloused hands over the wizard. Mullein closed his eyes and spoke from the very back of his throat. As the volume of his voice increased, the walls of the cavern seemed to vibrate.

"Speak no truths, my wizard, and hear no lies,
Your voice may utter, but your tongue is tied."

"There," Mullein said, his voice back to normal. "Now he can't call for help." He let out a deep, bellowing laugh as he started to walk away, towards the back of the cave. Little did he, or his siblings know, Magus already had called for help.

"Wait, my brother!" Bellis called out. "What do we do now?"

"Now," Mullein replied, "we wait for Celandine."

CHAPTER 2

"*Felix! Awaken, my love!*"

Eleonora's voice rang through her husband's ears, causing him to stir. "Not now," he mumbled. "The palace is under attack..."

"No, it isn't. You're dreaming," she replied. "Wake up, would you?"

Felix rolled over and pulled the blanket over his head. "My people need me."

Eleonora laughed. "Come on, honeysuckle. I have good news!"

Felix shot up. "You're pregnant?" His eyes were wide with excitement.

Eleonora laughed again, this time somewhat nervously. "Um, no. Sorry. That's not the news."

"No, I'm sorry. I shouldn't have jumped to that conclusion. It's just... you know how much I want..."

"I know, Felix. I do, too. But it will happen when the time is right. That's what your mother keeps telling me, anyway."

Now it was Felix's turn to laugh nervously. "Yeah, uh, sorry about that, sweet-cakes. You know how she is."

"It's okay, I don't mind. I just wish everyone would shut up about the baby thing for awhile, you know?"

"But not enough to speak up about it."

"Clearly not."

"Anyway, what's your exciting news? I'm wide awake now."

"My sister is coming to visit!"

Felix's face fell. "Isadora? I thought you didn't get along with her."

"What are you talking about? When did I say that?"

"Eleonora, you're always saying that Isadora needs to get it together."

Eleonora snorted. "That doesn't mean we don't get along."

"Wait, doesn't your sister have a child?"

"Yeah, Dorabella. *Don't* talk about the father, please. It's a sore subject."

"Not a problem. When are they getting here?"

"Today! The message was late, I guess. I just got it now, but they should be here before nightfall."

"What is going on with the messengers?" Felix asked, changing the subject. "That's at least the tenth failed or late message I've heard about in the last moon cycle. I need to look into this..."

Eleonora smiled at her husband, though looked slightly defeated. "Okay, I'm going to go prepare some rooms. Have a good day, honey."

Felix didn't reply. He was too busy getting dressed to see when Eleonora left, but did notice that she was gone by the time he was ready to begin his duties as Nymph King. Figuring she'd gone to ready the palace for her sister's visit, he thought nothing of it as he made his way down the hallway to the throne room, where he'd be briefed on his schedule for the day.

"Oh, don't worry," a familiar voice chuckled from the throne room as Felix entered. "You're *all* going to get eaten."

"Who's getting eaten?" Felix asked with a grin, approaching the black-haired, lavender-eyed troll who was seated sideways upon his throne, legs hanging over the arm rest. "Has your fierce gluttony finally gotten the best of you?"

Indeed, Felix had a point, though he was oblivious to the potentially hurtful implications of his careless comment. Myso *had* gotten fairly lazy since his time spent battling the ghouls and monsters of the Forest during the haunting. Nowadays, he mainly supervised the Nymph Kingdom's multi-species army, that is, when he wasn't hanging around the palace looking for Eleonora's caramel-coated crawlies. The Forest had a way of affecting its enchanted inhabitants; the elementals and animals that dwelt within were highly susceptible to its energies simply by residing there. When the Forest was out of balance—as it had been for some generations now—the little beings too became out of balance, and likewise more vulnerable to *any* influence within the ever-fluctuating aura of the land. It was the negative energies that were of the most concern, however, since those were known to inspire an overall sense of apathy—the most damaging of all.

"Yes, King Felix, my waistline has expanded. But it has made me a far more intimidating bodyguard for your royal highness, has it not?"

Felix laughed. "You'd better leave some crawlies for my niece. She's due to arrive later with her mother."

"Isadora?" Myso guffawed. "Good luck with that one! I've heard far too many stories..."

"As have I," Felix sighed. "We'll see it how it goes. Now, my good friend, would you mind?"

Myso grinned, stood up, and gave a long bow to the king. "Blessed be, my king. Enjoy your day, before Isadora gets here!" He sauntered out of the room.

Felix sat down on his throne, letting his body sink into the velvet, down feather pillows that had been hand sewn especially for him by his witch friend, Lorella. Soon after, Basil scurried into the room to place Felix's crown on his head before leaving to fetch the king breakfast.

Once he'd eaten, Felix waited patiently for the messengers of the day. When none arrived, he got up to investigate the matter himself.

"Strange," he said aloud, despite no one being around as he walked the halls of the palace. "Where is everybody?"

He went into his study. There sat Myso and Basil, in the sitting area by the window that looked over all of Nymph Kingdom. Their eyes were fixated out the window, and as Felix moved closer he saw that it was Eleonora that they were watching.

"Ah, off to pick up Isadora, I imagine?" Felix broke the silence.

Myso and Basil jerked slightly, as if Felix's sudden presence had startled them. "Yes, King Felix," they replied in unison.

"A bit early, isn't it?" Felix said.

"Eleonora was concerned that since the message was so late, that perhaps something had changed or the timing was somehow off," Basil replied. "She wanted to make sure that she was there the moment Isadora arrived."

"Something about Isadora being upset with her if she wasn't," Myso broke in. "Eleonora mumbled that on her way out the door."

"I wish I understood their dynamic more," Felix replied. "That's all I will say."

"What happened with the child's father?" Basil asked softly.

"All I know is that he left Isadora for whatever reason, but unfortunately, he has since passed. I do not know how."

"Perhaps that's why Isadora acts the way she does, from what I hear. We musn't judge her," Basil said.

"Not just yet, anyway," Myso chimed in with a wink.

"Oh! Speaking of messengers," Felix said. "I need you two to check the boundary lines of the kingdom. Something is clearly awry with the entrance of messengers, and it needs to be investigated before beings start to complain."

Myso chuckled. "They've been complaining already, for at least two moon cycles! I'm sure I've told you this, Your Highness. More than once."

"It must have slipped my mind, my dear friend," Felix replied. "I was not fully aware of this was until I awakened and Eleonora mentioned it. I apologize that it hadn't sunk in before."

"We have all been forgetting things, Felix," Basil said. "'Tis nothing to be ashamed of. It happens to the very best of us."

"We will do that right now," Myso broke in as Basil nodded fervently in accord. "No time to waste."

Myso and Basil immediately left to prepare themselves for their mission. Felix sat down in one of his chairs, confused as to why he'd forgotten about the messenger ordeal. He felt like his mind was playing tricks on him, like he was trapped within a thick cloud that impaired his thoughts. That feeling had been creeping up on him for quite some weeks now, inserting itself slowly into his thoughts. It was as if anything that involved logic or reasoning went flying out the window, and any thoughts that were self-deprecating or overly dramatic reigned supreme.

His dreams since the haunting, however, had always made perfect sense, and perhaps that was why it was so difficult for him to leave them.

The dreams had taken him to long forgotten, faraway lands where the pure essence of his purpose and existence seemed to belong. When he wasn't asleep, vivid memories of the dreams plagued his waking consciousness.

Even Eleonora had told him she'd noticed a change in him, one that started just after he'd returned from his apprenticeship with Sator. It was almost as if, to be the king of the nymphs, one had to slowly but surely lose oneself. It was as if fated—beyond one's control. Or was it?

"Felix!"

A soft, yet firm female voice called out to him. One that Felix was well acquainted with.

"Hello, Mother."

Felix got up from his seat to embrace Narena. His father, Kellen, and grandfather, Felide, stood behind her.

"Hello, Father. Hello, Grandfather. How are you all today?"

"Well, honestly son, we've been better," Narena replied.

"Ah, so you've heard about Isadora?"

The corners of Kellen's mouth lifted into a slight smile. "No, son. That's not what this is about."

"Do I have reason for concern?"

"Yes, Felix," Felide broke in. "Your mother has channeled some harrowing news during her morning meditation. She discovered..."

"The Controllers are back," Kellen interjected, his brow furrowed. "We need to secure the kingdom."

"What do you mean? Who are the Controllers?"

"Of course he hasn't heard of them, Kellen!" Narena said, sounding frustrated. "Their mere existences were struck from the Forest's written records!"

"Only those who are truly connected with the spiritual realm are likely aware of them," Felide said. "Narena's sage abilities allowed her to connect with Hawthorne, who told her about Magus's plight..."

"They've got him," Kellen interrupted his father again, this time causing Felide to purse his lips and take in a long, deep breath. "The Controllers have Magus. We have to save him."

"And do something about the Controllers," Felide continued. "Unfortunately, we only have access to very little knowledge about them, and even less information on how to defeat or cast them away again, as was done long, long ago."

"The Higher Spirits must have done it," Narena said bluntly. "We know that much. But without Labete now, and the Forest being so out of balance..."

"Magus told me once that he knew the Controllers," Kellen added. "And only that they were all siblings; ancient warlocks whose souls molded with that of their elemental realm. Supposedly, they got into a huge fight, caused the Under Spirits to get involved, messed up the whole Forest, possessed the ogres in order to control them—which got *them* cast out—and then, eventually, the Controllers were cast out themselves. They've been trapped within the darkest depths of their elemental realms for centuries."

"Until now, apparently," Felide finished. He paused for a moment before continuing, sharing a quick glance with Kellen. "Come to think of it, I'd heard the legends about an ancient coven as a child. I guess I just never thought they were anything more than scary stories to keep me awake at night and get me to do my chores." He chuckled a bit. "I suppose all legends are based somewhere in truth."

"The stories had long since turned to complete bear scat by the time they got to my generation," Kellen said. "I think there was even a poem...

"The Controllers: fire, earth, water, and air,
will come for you, if you don't beware.
They'll steal your life and possess your soul,
whether you're a faery, nymph, gnome, or troll."

"I've been saying that something is awry for endless moon cycles now!" Narena broke in. "Nobody ever listens to me!"

"What makes them warlocks, and not just witches and wizards?" Felide asked. "I've always wondered that."

"Warlocks have gone completely to the darkness," Narena replied. "I read once that the word 'warlock' is derived from an ancient word that translated to 'oath-breaker'. A warlock has deceived the Higher Spirits by turning to Gorgon and the Under Spirits, essentially duping the Higher Spirits into providing them with a boost to their magical abilities, only to turn around and defy them to join the ranks of Gorgon and his minions. Our friend Nessaba was once a warlock, from what I gather, but she had enough sense to return to the light."

"Ah, I never knew that," Felide replied, a smile curling around the corners of his mouth. "Thank you for your knowledge, Narena. As always."

"Then let's secure the kingdom!" Felix spoke finally. "Gather our troops. I would like to participate in this investigation personally."

"Yes, let's make haste!" Felide replied, motioning to the doorway.

As quickly as their little nymph legs could carry them, Felix, his parents, and his grandfather scurried out the door.

Myso and Basil headed toward the northernmost corner of Nymph Kingdom. They walked briskly, as the air and general aura of the Forest around them seemed ill, in the oddest sense. Neither spoke of the discord about them, yet they both were enveloped with the same feeling.

The afternoon sun was slowly descending from the sky, and the thought of the rapidly approaching dusk caused the troll and skunk to quicken their pace.

"We need to at least secure the northernmost border and make the guards aware of the messenger ordeal," Myso muttered.

"Yes, Myso," Basil replied between hurried breaths. "Then we can make our way south and stop off at the western ridge along the way."

"Isadora will be arriving to the kingdom soon, I imagine. Felix will likely be feeling the stress of his wife, not to mention the irritation that comes with having a youngster in the home."

"As long as everyone is considerate of everyone else, I would like to think that everything will be fine, just fine." Basil smiled, though unsure as to whether he felt hopeful or just desperate for harmony within the palace walls. Likely both, as Basil had always been one to desire balance in all aspects of his life. He was far more patient and understanding than any other skunk he'd ever met, and certainly more so than any faery or troll. But the nymphs—the sweet oblivious nymphs—they were the beings to rival the kindhearted skunk in any harrowing situation, and perhaps that's why Basil enjoyed living among them in Nymph Kingdom.

Myso, though often still plagued with the overwhelming emotions and short temper of his species, generally stayed positive through meditation, which he picked up in his time as a warrior. It had proved especially useful during the haunting.

Had all the species within the Forest realized the benefits of meditation, perhaps the Forest's plight would have been a much less distressing ordeal. But as it was, the Forest was terribly out of balance, and the fight or flight instinct inherent in all beings overpowered the land. Small revolutions within kingdoms were becoming common, and slowly but surely the beings of the Forest were collectively losing faith in their kingdoms, rulers, and even the Higher Spirits.

Myso and Basil saw the outline of the guard tower in the approaching horizon. As they grew nearer, they exchanged concerned looks. Both could feel a change in energy, prompting the lifelong friends to draw closer to one another, Myso's hand hovering over his blade and Basil's lips unconsciously curling over his gums. Something was off, and both were fully aware of it.

When they reached the tower, the two split up and circled the outside. Within its stone walls, there was only a winding wooden staircase that led to the lookout point at the top, which oversaw the majority of the northernmost end of Nymph Kingdom. Once the two met up once more, they headed upstairs.

"Is anyone up there?" Myso called. When there came no response, they continued their ascent.

The light of the sunset shone brightly in their faces as Myso and Basil finally reached the top, temporarily blinding them until their eyes were finally able to adjust to the change in lighting.

"Nobody's here..." Basil said softly, but Myso did not hear him.

In the corner behind the stairwell lay the body of a nymph, crumpled into an almost unrecognizable heap on the cold stone floor. Strangely enough, his blade was still secured within its holster, and it looked as though the poor soul hadn't even made an attempt to use it before he perished. A blackish-gray powder was dusted over the corpse and sprinkled around the sides in a pattern that Myso had never seen before, and therefore could not fully comprehend. To him, it looked like ancient magic—the kind of spell that was highly frowned upon in the Forest, and had been for many, many generations.

"So that's what's happening to the messengers, I guess..." he trailed off, not noticing that Basil had come right up beside him. "It's Leroy, I'm afraid."

"Oh dear," Basil whispered. "This is a problem, isn't it?"

"Black magic," Myso said. "It almost looks like... volcanic ash, or something."

"I wouldn't know," Basil replied. "The only ash I've ever seen like that was the remnants of our foes during the time of the haunting. And not every foe—just one, Vulcan. The ash from the other underworld monsters looked a bit different from his, as I recall. Not much different... only slightly."

"Well, ash is the result of fire. If it is indeed volcanic ash, there's only one place it could have come from."

"The beast we battled during the haunting?"

"Well, he came from the underworld, didn't he? He had to have been created somewhere. The very place this ash came from."

"Where is that?"

"The Fire Realm. But not the part of the Fire Realm where the salamanders reside. I think it came from the darkest part of the Fire Realm, close to the entrance to the underworld."

"Does that mean there's another Vulcan creature in our Forest?"

Myso let out a nervous laugh. "We could only be so lucky." He exhaled deeply before continuing to speak, this time in a low voice. "My gut tells me whoever did this is much, much worse than the Vulcan."

"An Under Spirit?"

"Not exactly. Look here, Basil." Myso twirled his finger in the air above the corpse, tracing the pattern for Basil. "The ash is not strewn haphazardly—as it would be if it had fallen from a beast's body at random during an attack. Instead, the ash is formed in a deliberate, unrecognizable pattern, at least to us beings of light. Now, what does that tell us?"

"That it's likely a spell?"

"Precisely." Myso turned to face Basil. "But now the question is: what kind of spell was it?"

"Uh, Myso?" Basil asked, his voice now shaky.

"Yes?" Myso replied.

"Is he supposed to be getting up?"

"Who?"

"The nymph!"

"The nymph? The dead nymph? Well, of course not! That would defeat the whole purpose of him being dead, wouldn't it?"

Basil raised one of his paws, his pointer claw outstretched. "Then why is he?!"

Myso whipped around, only to come face to face with the sullen, bloodshot eyes of the dead male nymph. The nymph opened its mouth, maggots pouring from within, and breathed rotten, stinking moisture right into the troll's face.

"What happened to you, Nymph?" Myso asked, his heart pounding. "Who did this to you?"

The nymph smiled creepily, dragging his dried, leathery lips over his now-decaying teeth. He said nothing at first, but after a moment, he ground his jaw back and forth, chattering his teeth while also somehow bellowing out a deep, unsettling laugh.

"The lady says I cannot speak,
Unless it's to the souls I reap.
For eternity, I'll feast on flesh,
until I am like all the rest..."

"Myso, what is that supposed to mean?" Basil hissed.

"He's a zombie..." was all Myso could reply before the undead nymph lunged straight for his throat.

CHAPTER 3

Eleonora scurried down the deer path that led to the outskirts of Nymph Kingdom. For some reason, the quick journey to retrieve her sister and niece was taking far longer than she anticipated. Isadora and Dorabella would be arriving in nymph territory from the east, in the direction of Faery Kingdom. The sky had grown dark what seemed like ages ago, and though there was still a hint of glow from the waning moonlight, Eleonora couldn't suppress the unsettling feeling that was inching its way from her belly to her throat. The "witching hour" was near, where the sky would be at its darkest and no hint of light from the moon would make itself visible. Nothing good occurred during that time period. If one was smart, one was fast asleep for the witching hour.

It wasn't that times associated with all witches were considered bad, but the few who practiced black magic had associated even good witches with the negative connotations of the witching hour. Eleonora was quite familiar with the good witches of the Elder Triage, but had heard far too many stories of the wicked kind to walk the Forest at night with the utmost of confidence.

"I need a torch," she whispered to herself, her legs shaking a bit. "Soon I won't be able to see at all."

Her eyes scanned the Forest in front of her, and landed on a twig that was thick on one end and skinny on the other. It would be perfect for a torch. Now for the fire...

Eleonora crouched on the ground and ran her hand around the bottom of a tree for some suitable tinder. She gathered the driest bits she could find, setting just a few pieces aside for the start of her fire, and secured them to the thick end of her twig with some tree sap.

"I need just a small piece of obsidian," she muttered. "Spirits of the Forest, please oblige and I will be forever indebted to you."

She crawled on her hands and knees to the other side of the towering oak tree, her eyes never lifting from the Forest floor. She squinted, barely able to see, but pressed forward another few fox tail's lengths. Her hand suddenly touched something hard and smooth, but when she tried to grab it, she found it was far too hot to touch.

"What is this?" she said aloud, tapping the object a few times. It was as if it were on fire, yet not fully aflame. "How curious..." Eleonora whispered.

"Ahem," a female voice bellowed from above.

Eleonora jumped, and her eyes shot upward.

A woman, cloaked in red, stood directly above the wingless faery, her arms folded as if annoyed by something. She had a strikingly beautiful face, with prominent cheekbones and a pointed, pin-straight nose. Her hair—a red-orange ensemble of curls and wisps—cascaded down her front in generous locks. Her eyes were piercing and unforgiving, somewhere between a deep burgundy and blood-stained brown. Strangely enough, she seemed familiar to Eleonora, but not enough to distract the little Nymph Queen from the disturbing feeling she was getting just by looking upon the looming woman.

"I beg your pardon, my lady," Eleonora said, projecting her soft voice upwards despite a lump in her throat. "I seem to have overstepped my way."

"You are forgiven," the lady replied, her voice strong and curt. She looked down at Eleonora, and a spark of interest briefly danced in her eyes. "Now, tell me, what is such a small, innocent being as yourself doing in such a big, bad, scary Forest? You know it's almost the hour of darkness, yes?"

"Please, my lady, I must be on my way. Forgive my intrusion."

The woman smiled, and though it was quite beautiful, it was also quite eerie, as if somehow void of emotion. "I can't just leave you out here like this." She bent to her knees, lowered her head to peer directly into Eleonora's cerulean eyes, and whispered, "The monsters are afoot."

Eleonora gulped.

The woman pulled herself up in one sweeping motion, like a flame popping up the wick of a candle, and laughed heartily. "It must be your lucky night, because I'm feeling generous at the moment. I haven't been able to walk properly in Gorgon-knows-how-long, and I must admit, it feels good. Now, what is your name, my dear?"

Eleonora's thoughts were frantic. The woman seemed nice now, but she couldn't shake her initial feelings of unease. If there was one thing that Eleonora had learned from becoming a member of Felix's family, it was to always trust your intuition. Narena told her that almost every day, and time and time again, she had been proven right. Eleonora knew this was not the time to ignore her feelings and give this woman the benefit of the doubt. Something was off about her, and Eleonora didn't want to stick around to find out what it was.

"My name?" Eleonora stammered. "My name is, um... Esmeralda."

The woman's eyes narrowed, but then drifted down to the unlit torch in Eleonora's hand. She cocked her head, pursed her lips, and intensely focused her eyes. The torch burst into flames, roaring through the tinder and causing Eleonora to frantically grab as many twigs and leaves as she could to prevent it from burning out as quickly as it had started.

The woman smiled eerily once again. "Like I mentioned before, tonight I'm feeling generous."

Eleonora knew enough about the differences between modern and ancient magic to know that what just happened was a nearly impossible feat in this day and age. That type of instantaneous spell was not unheard of, but at present she knew of no one within the Forest—being, animal, or human witch—who was powerful enough to cast such a spell at will, without the proper incantation or ritual. Aside from the Higher and Under Spirits that were left, nobody wielded the tremendous amount of magical power needed to control an element in such a way. These realizations only made Eleonora more terrified of the woman, and she was determined to get away—whether the woman was genuine in her intentions or not.

"Thank you, my lady," Eleonora said as sincerely as she could. "Your kindness will aid in my journey, but I really must go." She turned to leave.

"Very well," the woman replied bluntly. "Oh, and Esmeralda?"

Eleonora reluctantly turned back. "Yes?"

"You may consider yourself lucky on this night for another reason."

"Why is that?"

"You will be the only being in this Forest who will encounter me and live to speak of it."

Eleonora took off running once she was sure that the sinister woman could no longer see her. Her torch burned bright and forceful as ever, never waning once as she weaved through the bramble patch that grew down the length of Faery Kingdom. The patch was added during the most recent generation—planted shortly after King Laurel died under mysterious circumstances. His son and heir to the crown, Lucian, had decided the kingdom could cut down on unwanted travelers (or "tick-gypsies", as the faeries called them) who were just passing through. After the haunting, the Faery Kingdom had made it abundantly clear to all the kingdoms of the Forest that they valued their sanctity and privacy above all else, and all tourism to Faery Kingdom would need to be approved by the council. The endless wall of bramble bushes caused a blockage that prompted most animals and beings—in need of rest or not—to continue on their way rather than braving the thorns to seek refuge with the faeries.

Eleonora was just about to look behind a particularly large, thorny bush, when she heard her name echo across the leaves that formed an umbrella-shaped canopy over her head. The voice was familiar, though not in the same way that the strange woman's voice had been. This voice, to Eleonora, sounded oddly comforting, and yet at the same time, also made her stomach drop.

"Oh, sister! Do you even hear me?"

Eleonora turned around to see Isadora fluttering towards her, her eyes wide and sparkling lavender. She wore a shimmering green dress with a wispy skirt that trailed behind her like a turbulent wave on the ocean. Her hair was almost black, with lighter, chestnut-brown highlights to match her sister's, though wavy and shoulder-length. Behind her, a smaller, lighter-featured faery bumbled about, looking as though she were trying to catch up. As the tiny faery grew closer, Eleonora began to smile.

"Auntie Nora!" the little faery squealed in delight.

"Dorabella!" Eleonora called back. "I can't believe how big you've grown!"

Isadora and her daughter stopped in front of Eleonora and slowly descended to the ground. Dorabella ran to her aunt and wrapped her arms around her waist, burying her face in her stomach.

"But my eyes have stayed the same, look!" Dorabella lifted her head to dramatically bat her eyelashes at Eleonora, who laughed.

"Yes, of course! Same color as mine!"

"What about my eyes?" Isadora interrupted. "Mine haven't changed, either."

"And neither have you, my dear sister."

"Same to you."

The two female faeries furrowed their brows at one another for a moment, before bursting into uncontrollable laughter and embracing.

"What are you doing here so late?" Isadora said as they pulled away. "Such a strange hour to be out and about, don't you think?"

"I could ask you the same thing," Eleonora replied. "And you're out here with my little Dora."

"We came out looking for you," Isadora said hurriedly. "I was getting worried."

"Of course you were," Eleonora snorted with a playful wink.

"When are we going to your house, Auntie Nora?" Dorabella broke in. "Mommy says you get to live in a palace because you decided to marry down."

Eleonora wrinkled her nose. "What's that supposed to mean?"

"Ha, ha," Isadora said, putting her hand over her daughter's mouth. "That's a joke."

Eleonora felt her face grow hot. If she were a less considerate being, she might have spoken aloud any of the defensive retorts that were swirling around in her mind. But Eleonora generally preferred to avoid confrontation of any nature, especially with individuals with whom she preferred to have a peaceful relationship—even if that meant she took a few blows to her own ego in the process.

"Well, my darling," Eleonora said, avoiding eye contact with her sister, "we can go right now, if you're ready."

"Aren't you tired from all that walking?" Isadora asked with a frown. "I guess you can rest here for awhile if you need to..."

"I'll be fine," Eleonora assured, recalling the eerie woman. "I'm wide awake."

"Let me grab my satchel!" Dorabella replied, taking off towards the entrance to her kingdom. "I'll be right back!"

"Grab mine too, would you sweetie?" Isadora called after her.

"Got it!" the little faery yelled back, her voice drifting further away.

Isadora turned to her sister. "You know that's just a joke, right? About marrying down."

Eleonora mustered a slight smile. "Of course, Izzy. I know you wouldn't insult my husband, King of the Nymphs, unless it was just in good fun."

"And you are Queen of the Nymphs, despite the fact that you aren't one."

"You seem to forget I was appointed to my position *by* the nymphs."

"Because Felix was clearly enamored with you."

Eleonora sighed. "Whatever the reason, Izzy, I *am* Queen of the Nymphs now. I certainly didn't choose to be, and I am obviously not a nymph. So I'm not sure what else you want me to say."

"Say nothing, Nora, for that is your specialty."

Eleonora remained quiet, and the two stood in silence for what seemed like an eternity. Finally, Dorabella arrived breathing heavily, with a small satchel over her shoulder, and dragging a second, much larger satchel behind her.

"Let me help you with that." Eleonora hurried to the child and took the bag from her. It had to have weighed as much as a full-grown buck. "Here," she said, using all her strength to hand the satchel to her sister. "You pack, you carry."

Isadora scrunched her nose in disapproval. "But I didn't pack it myself."

Eleonora groaned and started to walk away, with Dorabella trailing behind her.

"Come on, Mommy!" the child yelled.

Isadora exhaled loudly and rolled her eyes, looking helplessly from her satchel to her family, who were now heading further and further into the Forest, disappearing from view. "Wait for me!" she called, swinging her bag over her back and practically knocking herself over in the process. By the time Isadora had caught up to Eleonora and Dorabella, she was completely out of breath.

"You shouldn't pack so much, Mommy," Dorabella said.

"Mommy needs a lot of stuff," Isadora replied between gasps for air.

"You're only staying for one moon cycle," Eleonora said. "You can't possibly need everything in that bag."

"How would you know?" Isadora snapped. "You don't know what I need on a daily basis."

"What one needs is relative, I suppose," Eleonora backed off.

"Well..." Isadora said, "I... should... tell... you..."

"Here." Eleonora took the satchel from her sister and swung it over her own back. "It's actually a lot lighter once you get used to carrying the weight."

"Ha, ha, let's all laugh at the weak little faery," Isadora remarked, looking irritated.

"I'm not laughing! I thought I was helping, but if you don't want me to, I won't!"

"I do want your help!" Isadora said. "In fact, that's why I'm visiting in the first place!"

"Oh, this is new," Eleonora replied. "What help do you need from me now?"

"We're moving in with you!" Dorabella interjected happily. "Mommy says we get to live the palace forever now!"

Eleonora stopped dead in her tracks.

CHAPTER 4

yso leaped out of the way right before the zombie's drool-covered teeth sank into his neck, swinging his blade wildly in front of him. It sliced across the zombie nymph's midsection, spilling his entrails to the cold, stone floor at the top of the lookout tower. The zombie did not halt his advance, however, and continued his pursuit of the troll, sloshing through a pile of his own organs and body fluid in the process.

Out of nowhere, Basil charged at the zombie nymph, swiping his claws through the air. He slashed the nymph across the throat, causing his head to tilt, then finally fall backwards. The zombie nymph groaned and swirled around in a circle, trying to right his head back upon his rotting shoulders.

"You have to finish it!" Myso yelled. "He'll keep coming until he's headless! You must sever his spine at the neck or compromise the brain!"

Basil swung his right paw at the nymph, cutting through the final piece of flesh to send the zombie's head tumbling to the ground. It rolled a short distance, then stopped to rest upon what remained of its neck, the eyes pointed directly upwards at Myso's shocked expression.

"Forgive me, my friend, I must've forgotten you had it in you to do that," he mumbled.

"I just wanted to make him equal in appearance to you, my dear troll."

Myso turned to his friend and chuckled, jovially knocking him with his elbow. "Come on now, let's go home! Felix must hear of this as soon as possible."

"Indeed," Basil said. "Let's be on our way."

Myso started to walk away, then paused. "Wait," he said.

Basil stopped in his tracks. "What is it?" he asked.

"Shouldn't we take some of this ash with us?" Myso motioned to the scattered remains of the ash pattern that was laid out before the zombie nymph reanimated. "We should have somebody take a look at it."

"Like Magus?" Basil said. "We could stop at the home of the Elder Triage on our way back to Nymph Kingdom."

"I'm afraid we don't have time for that. Something tells me that this is really bad..."

"I fear my gut agrees with you. Perhaps Narena can lend some insight."

"You're right, Basil. Let's go."

Myso retrieved a small bag from his warrior satchel and scooped a good-sized portion of the ash into it before heading down the staircase, Basil following closely behind.

The two walked for quite some time, following a commonly-traveled deer path that would lead them back to Nymph Kingdom. As they passed the Bee Kingdom, Myso suddenly had an idea.

"We should get a bee messenger to tell Felix about the zombie nymph," he said, his heels practically skidding to a halt at the brilliance of his realization. "That way, we can take the ash to Magus and the witches. We can even send a tiny bit of ash with the bee so Narena can take a look at it as well."

"I think that's a great idea, Myso," Basil replied. "Let's see if we can get a bee to help us out."

Myso and Basil headed into Bee Kingdom, passing through the seemingly endless rows of honeysuckle and lavender bushes that weaved around a congregation of young oak trees. The euphoric smell overtook their sensitive nostrils, enveloping their entire bodies in a sweet aroma that caused them to almost blindly drift on wisps of air through the passageway and into the clearing where Bee Kingdom began.

Globular hives were secured to any bush or tree that was strong enough, dripping sticky golden honey that oozed from the entryways. Hundreds, if not thousands of bees flew in and out of the hives, following some kind of rhythmic pattern as they zipped along invisible traffic lanes. The buzzing sound was loud and penetrated Myso's ears, as if it were some kind of meditation that reverberated in his mind and heightened his vibrations. It was as if Bee Kingdom had a vibration of its own, a pulse that caused the heart to beat somewhere deep within the Forest's core.

"How do we get their attention?" Basil whispered.

"What?" Myso shouted, cupping his ear to point towards the skunk.

"I said, *HOW DO WE GET THEIR ATTENTION?*"

The buzzing stopped. Myso looked up to see that the bees—every single one of them—had halted in mid-air and were now all staring at him.

Myso cleared his throat loudly. "Um, hello bees! I am Myso, warrior of Nymph Kingdom, and this is Basil, also a warrior. We are here to seek your assistance in an urgent matter, I'm afraid."

All of Bee Kingdom instantly erupted in what sounded like a low humming noise, but when Myso truly concentrated, he could make out what individual bees were saying in response to his request.

"Bzz bzz, he's a nymph?"

"But he looks like a troll."

"Why are they from Nymph Kingdom?"

"What's going on?! Bzz bzz."

"Is that skunk going to eat us?"

"I'll sting 'em if you want, Queen!"

"Yes, we'll all sting them."

"Wait!" Myso interjected loudly. "Don't sting us! Please, we really need your help."

"Can we at least speak with your queen before you sting us?" Basil asked.

The sound burst forth again.

"The queen said not to help outsiders anymore."

"We don't help beings we don't know anymore."

"There aren't many of us left, we have to be careful now."

"The faeries think we should just keep to ourselves."

"The queen said she didn't want to be bothered today."

"The queen will not want to speak with you."

Myso sighed loudly. "All right then, bees. If you will not help us then I'm afraid we must bid you our gratitude and be on our way."

The bees said nothing, and instead continued on their pathways as if nothing had ever happened. Myso turned to Basil and shrugged.

"I guess we're on our own, then."

"Wait," a tiny voice buzzed.

Myso and Basil turned to see a bee much smaller than the ones they had just been speaking to, probably only half the size of the largest one.

She fluttered closer, and hovered between the two warriors.

"You are quite small," Myso muttered as he studied the little bee. "But then again, when has that ever prevented one from succeeding in the task at hand?" He crouched down so the hymenopteran floated directly in front of his face. "What is your name, little one?"

"It's Druzy, sir," the bee replied, her voice somewhere between a squeak and a buzz. *"How can I help you?"*

"Let's go out here, where we can hear each other better," Myso said, and Basil nodded fervently.

The three walked and flew back out through the entrance to Bee Kingdom, stopping once the humming sound was far enough away.

"All right, Druzy," Myso began. "We need you to deliver a message to King Felix in Nymph Kingdom. Let me just write it out for you. If you don't mind, could you also deliver a letter to the mother of the king? She is at the palace as well..." He trailed off as he fiddled around in his satchel before finally pulling out a small scroll of paper and feather-tip pen, the quill of the feather filled with indigo berry ink. He began writing furiously, and when he was finished, he tore off part of the paper, folded it three times, and wrote *Felix* on it. Then he scribbled on the scroll for another quick moment, transferred a tiny bit of the ash to the center of the note, wrapping the note around the ash and then folding it closed, and wrote *Narena*. He handed the notes to Druzy.

"You'll be able to carry them both without trouble, right?" he asked the bee.

"Of course, sir," Druzy buzzed. *"Where shall I find you to tell you the notes have been delivered?"*

"At the home of the Elder Triage. Just buzz around the windows. We'll be keeping an eye out for you."

"Bzz, Elder Triage? My queen says we are forbidden to go there."

"Why is that?" Basil broke in. "Does your queen not know that the witches are good?"

"She cares not if the witches are good—all humans are bad," Druzy replied bluntly. *"Humans are the reason that my kind are almost gone."*

"I give you my word, Druzy, that the human witches of the Elder Triage cannot—and will not—harm you in any way. I promise," Myso declared confidently.

"We are indebted to you for helping us," Basil added. "The witches are our friends, they have been for over a generation. They will not harm you or your kind."

Druzy hesitated. *"But... but I could be banished for disobeying my queen... but... but... I will do it anyway. It seems important."*

"It is! Very important," Basil said. "Thank you so much!"

"Please, Druzy, make haste!" Myso said as the bee started to take off. "And if you see any zombies... run!"

But Druzy did not hear him, for she was not only the littlest bee in her colony, but she was also the fastest. Whether or not she was aware of it, that would be for her to discover in her own lifetime.

Felix, Kellen, and Felide had gathered the multi-species Nymph Army and stationed them around every inch of the kingdom's perimeter. If any being, animal, or even spirit were to so much as graze past Nymph Kingdom's energetic field, Felix would become aware of it. Nightfall was rapidly approaching, so torches were lit and softly-spoken prayers to the

Higher Spirits were whispered to the night sky. Felide had just rolled the last cannon into position when the sun's light disappeared entirely, and darkness quickly swept through the canopy, completely overtaking the trees.

A tiny bee, her buzz barely even audible, tore through a thick patch of oak trees, knocking leaves and twigs in all directions as she flew. She burst off the deer path and headed straight for Felix.

"King Felix! Bzz bzz," the bee called frantically. *"King Felix, I have a message from a troll and skunk!"*

Felix stopped, eyes wide, and accepted the message from the bee. "Thank you," he said. "What's that other note you have?"

"It's for a 'Narena'," Druzy replied. "Do you know where I might find her?"

"In the palace," Kellen called from a ways away. He'd always had exceptional hearing, something that Narena considered to be both a blessing and a curse.

"Right, got it," buzzed Druzy. *"Thank you sir!"* And with that, she took off towards the palace.

Felix opened the message and read it for a moment. He lifted his head with fury, brows furrowed. "My mother was right," he declared. "This is major cause for concern, indeed. Father!"

"Yes, my son?" Kellen replied, having rushed to his son's side after seeing his reaction to the message.

"I must go back to the palace. You and Grandfather stay here."

"What's going on that Father and I should be aware of?"

"Leroy was murdered at the east tower. Looks like it was done ritually, but unlike any kind of ritual we've seen during our time in the Forest. Myso and Basil are going to the Elders to obtain more information on the matter, and find out how to proceed. They will be heading back here when they're done, so be ready for their arrival."

"Very good, my king," Kellen said with a bow.

"Thank you, Father," Felix replied. Though he was indeed king, he'd always felt strange about his parents and grandfather being subordinate to him. He'd always had the utmost respect for the nymphs that essentially gave him life and made him who he was. No amount of power, prestige, or wealth could ever take that away in his eyes.

Felix embraced his father, and then his grandfather, before rushing back to the palace. There, his mother Narena was waiting for him in his study, seated upon one of the velvet armchairs. As Felix came closer, he saw that she was holding a small piece of paper, folded up, in her hand.

"Is that the ash?" he asked as he hurried to her side.

"Indeed," Narena replied, opening the paper for Felix to see. "I think I know what, or who, it's from, but I'm really hoping that I'm wrong, because if I am indeed right, then that means..."

"Who is it from, Mother?"

"Um, well, if I am correct in assuming that it came from the place I think it came from, then that would mean it came from the person I think it came from... Does that make sense?"

"No," Felix said. "Not one bit, I'm afraid."

Narena let out a deep sigh. "All right. Well, then. I'm pretty sure this ash is from one of the Controllers. And not just any Controller... from Celandine."

"Celandine?"

"She rules the Fire Realm. She's..." Narena let out a bout of nervous laughter before continuing, "the most powerful and dangerous of them all."

"Is she who we need to watch out for?"

"She's one of four that we need to watch out for. And she's the worst one, if my research is correct. She's the one who got them all cast out in the first place. She's—supposedly—the one who incited her siblings to hypnotize all the ogres, making them crazy and getting them all killed. That's if we were even to believe that all the ogres in existence were, in fact, entirely wiped out. It's possible that some may have survived, though I truly hope that I am wrong about that. It wasn't until Nessaba stepped in..."

"Let's not give her more credit than she deserves," Felix interrupted. "She is, after all, of the darkness."

"You're right," Narena replied. "We can't give her more power. Yew knows she already has enough black magic at her fingertips... literally."

"Is there anything I can do to help?"

Felix turned to see the messenger bee perched on one of his library's bookshelves, near the Elemeportal. It came as no surprise, since his mother had always been a friend to the animals of the Forest. Felix assumed Narena had invited the bee to rest for awhile before embarking on her journey home.

"Druzy, you should return to your kingdom," Narena interjected. "This is no place for a youngster."

"You should know better than anybody that size, age, and gender mean nothing in times of need, bzz bzz," Druzy replied with a grin as Narena's eyes widened in puzzlement at the little bee's forwardness. *"And yes, Narena, I know of all your accomplishments in the Forest's fight. I want to join you! Please!"*

"But from what you just told me a moment ago, your kind would be against it."

"I've never fit in with my kind. I've survived this long on stories and my own

daydreams of living in Nymph Kingdom. I may have been born a bee, but I certainly have never felt like one. And though I cannot change my appearance, I would like to change my surroundings. The nymphs are more accepting of others' differences than any other species, and I know you accept warriors of different species in your army. Even if I am not suited as a warrior, I'd still like to relocate to your kingdom. That is, if you'll have me."

"The bees have never sent us warriors," Felix broke in. "But I would hate to send you back to a place that you do not feel is your home. My wife felt similarly, and I would be doing her a disservice if I were to force your return."

"Thank you, my king," Druzy gushed. *"I promise I won't let you down!"*

"I'm sure you won't," Felix replied with a smile before turning to his mother. "I think we should go to the Elder Triage, too, and meet up with Myso and Basil."

"I agree, my son," Narena replied. "But we must leave at once, for they've likely already arrived there. I have an idea." She walked over to where Druzy was sitting. "Let's take the Elemeportal, shall we?"

Felix hesitated. "The last time I took the Elemeportal, I ended up at the coast. I feel like we could get there faster if we found a fox or deer to ride."

"Even if we took the fastest animal in the Forest, we could still miss them, and have to come all the way back here. What if we end up needing to go back to the witches again? Let's just take the Elemeportal, the Earth button will take us to the unincorporated area of the Forest." She paused, a wide grin stretched across her face. "Want to know the funniest part of this? If your father and I had known about the Elemeportal during the falling, we could have saved so much time."

"Mother, the only way I am taking that Elemeportal is if we bring an animal who we could ride on in the event that we end up further away than intended."

"Fair enough."

"I'll go ask the general to send a soldier to us," Druzy buzzed, and shot out the window. A few moments later, she flew back in the room. *"Felide is sending a fox."*

Felix and Narena prepared some satchels to leave, and shortly thereafter Kellen, accompanied by a husky gray fox with bright periwinkle eyes who introduced himself as Earl, joined them.

"Father, didn't I order you to remain with Grandfather?"

Kellen let out a sigh under his breath. "Grandfather will be just fine with the rest of the army. My talents are best utilized in action," was all he said. Now it was Felix's turn to sigh, though he released a much more exasperated one. "Besides," Kellen went on, "I need to protect my wife." Felix said nothing in reply.

"I'll come with you," Druzy offered. *"Just in case you need the extra set of wings. I can always return to the palace if needed."* Kellen nodded somberly in reply.

The three nymphs stood in front of the Elemeportal and climbed onto Earl's back. Narena stood up, Kellen holding her steady by the waist, and as Felix grabbed onto her ankles, she reached up and pushed the button for the Earth Realm, which had a picture of a deer etched into it.

A swirling vortex opened and swept the fox's whole body into its vacuum, pulling them through the wormhole of glimmering lights and glittering mist as they all clutched tightly to the thick fur on Earl's back. Once they made it through the vortex, the fox began to rapidly free-fall into the brightest white light that any of the beings had ever seen.

Chapter 5

"You're joking, right?" Eleonora said, her face scrunched in displeasure. "Ha, ha."

"Believe me," Isadora replied. "I wish it were a joke. I was just hoping we wouldn't have to discuss this until we were at least halfway there."

Eleonora's eyes followed her niece as she ran ahead of the two adult faeries. For a brief moment, Eleonora longed for the innocence she once had when she was Dorabella's age. So carefree, so void of concern, just knowing that someone—anyone—was going to be caring for you no matter what. True, the Forest was once a simpler place, but that shouldn't mean that the youngsters of the kingdoms had to suffer. In times of war and destruction, however, innocence was only a veil thrown over the heartbreaking realities with which all beings would become acquainted with, sooner or later. While Eleonora wished for those simpler times again, she knew deep down that they were as far gone as the set of wings she once wore upon her back.

"So what do you say, my sister?" Isadora's voice pierced through Eleonora's thoughts. "Can we live with you for awhile? Or are you going to heartlessly send us back to Faery Kingdom, where we've been shunned for her--" she motioned to Dorabella, "father's indiscretions?"

"I know nothing of that," Eleonora replied. "The faeries like to keep their personal matters just that—personal. You know I have been shunned too, right?"

"But you came out on top," Isadora went on. "You're a queen now." She paused, as if thinking over her words carefully before continuing, "Even though you're queen of the nymphs. At least you're still a queen, and treated as such."

Eleonora grunted before repeating her sister's words. "Even though I'm queen of the *nymphs*." She shook her head in disapproval. "If you really knew anything of the nymphs and their history, my sister, you would not speak such harsh words of my kind."

"Your kind?!" Isadora snorted. "Whatever you've become in your time spent with the nymphs, you must always remember: you were born a faery, Eleonora. I think the crown has squeezed too tightly around your skull."

Eleonora felt her face heat up again. She took a long, deep breath, but said nothing to her sister. She was trying to think of the perfect retort when she felt a small, warm hand slip into hers as she walked.

"Don't listen to my mommy," Dorabella whispered. Eleonora's eyes welled up with tears, despite her best efforts to blink them away. "She can be mean sometimes. I think that's why my daddy left."

"Well, I'm just glad *you're* here," Eleonora whispered back after she'd gathered her composure for a moment. "I can't wait to spend some time with you. I even have a batch of caramel-coated crawlies that I made yesterday. That is, if Myso hasn't devoured them all before we get back!"

Dorabella laughed. "Yum! Those are my favorite!"

"Mine, too," Eleonora said.

"Ugh! Are we almost there?!" Isadora whined from a few fox tail's lengths ahead. "My feet hurt."

"Then feel free to use your wings, my dear sister," Eleonora replied curtly. "By all means, don't allow my lack of flight prevent you from utilizing your Yew-given gifts to their full potential."

"Then I shall," Isadora said quickly. "I was trying to be nice by walking, since you're wingless and all."

"But I am still a queen," Eleonora muttered under her breath. And that was good enough for her, at least for now.

"According to my map, we should be at Nymph Kingdom by nightfall," Dorabella said, gesturing to a tiny map she'd pulled from her satchel.

"A map?! Where'd you get that?" Eleonora exclaimed. "I've never seen one that looked like that."

"She drew it herself," Isadora broke in. "She's really quite talented."

"I can see that," Eleonora said. "Dora, how were you able to create that? You must have spent hours in your king's library!"

"I did," Dorabella replied happily. "I took bits and pieces of all the maps depicted in the books. It's funny how they're all different, like from all the kingdom's perspectives. You'd think they'd all be the same, but they're not."

"Hmm," Eleonora said, trying to wrap her mind around that idea. For some reason, it didn't make sense to her.

"I think it has to do with some of the smaller disputes over land when these books were written," Isadora tried to explain. "I'm sure everybody in the Forest sees the boundaries properly now."

Eleonora snorted. That didn't sound right to her, but then again, when did *anything* Isadora say make sense? If Isadora had been conscious at all of the past generations, she would be well aware that not only were spiritual boundaries completely broken down in most—if not all—of the Forest, but most of the kingdom-based boundaries were following suit in the present day. Species—like the salamanders—were now completely extinct if not well on their way, and beings were distancing themselves because of discrimination based on completely unwarranted fears of other species.

Perhaps it was only the faeries that were truly jaded about the Forest's dark transformation. Eleonora could not recall anything in her time spent in Nymph Kingdom that justified the faeries' means. In times of trouble, beings should be standing together as one against the darkness, should they not?

"Is that who I think it is?" a thundering voice penetrated Eleonora's mind. Her eyes immediately darted to the scenery ahead of her.

In the path, standing tall and proudly, was a husky troll with jet-black hair and striking lavender eyes. He was jumping up and down, waving his arms frantically through the air while a curious-looking striped skunk sat in a pile of moss to his right.

"Eleonora!" the troll shouted. "My queen, is that you?"

Eleonora allowed a grin to slowly overtake her face. "Myso?"

The troll raced towards the three faeries, skidding to a halt in front of Eleonora. "My queen," he said softly with a sweeping bow. "How are you?"

"Could be better, could be worse. You know, the usual," Eleonora beamed at Myso before turning her eyes to the approaching skunk. "Basil, my dear. How utterly serendipitous to have run into you two. Where are you headed?"

"You wouldn't believe us even if we told you," Basil said.

"Oh, try me," Eleonora replied, chuckling.

"Did you eat all the caramel-coated crawlies?" Dorabella broke in, tugging on the bottom of Myso's tunic. He turned his attention downwards and smiled.

"Of course not!" he said jovially. "I left them all for you."

"Yeah, right," Eleonora snorted. "All two of 'em. Myso, Basil—this is my sister Isadora, and my niece, Dorabella."

"Pleasure," Myso said, shaking Dorabella's tiny hand.

"How delightful," Basil added. "We've heard many good things."

"I'm sure you have," Isadora muttered.

"Anyway," Eleonora said. "What happened with you guys?"

"A bit of a mishap, I'm afraid," Basil started.

"Poor old Leroy has passed on. And there was somewhat of an attack on the north tower," Myso finished.

"Somewhat of an attack?"

"Uh, yes. We've sent a messenger bee back to Felix, and now we are on our way to the home of the Elder Triage. We feel as though they may be able to explain more about the attack itself..."

"Why is that?"

"Well, the attack was unlike any we've ever seen."

"Come on, Myso. Your explanations are about as sugar-coated as the crawlies you love so much. I need real details, now. Please!" Eleonora hadn't meant to sound as frustrated as she did, but perhaps she was more on edge than usual. And after hearing about an attack where a nymph had perished, well, that was more unsettling to hear than the news of her sister's new residence in her home.

"Let me fill in some gaps," Basil piped up. "Here's a rundown of what happened: Myso and I reached the tower and discovered that Leroy had been killed. As we were investigating how and why, he suddenly woke up…"

"What?! He woke up? How?"

"Hang on here just a moment, Your Highness," Basil continued. "So, Leroy was now a zombie. He viciously attacked Myso, but we fought back and," he gulped, "finished him off, unfortunately."

"Well, it sounds like you had to. I'm glad you guys are all right, though my heart aches for poor Leroy and his family."

"As do ours," Basil said softly.

"We stopped by Bee Kingdom to procure a messenger to tell Felix of the matter, and luckily we were able to find a bee who would help us."

"Hmm. That's strange," Eleonora said. "I would think they would all be rallying to help…"

"Apparently not anymore," Basil replied. "The bees are going the way of the faeries. They'd like to be left alone, to their own kind."

"I don't blame them," Isadora grumbled from the side, but it seemed as though everyone chose to ignore her comment.

"But we were able to secure a young bee named Druzy for the job," Myso said. "And now, Queen Eleonora, I'm afraid we must be on our way if we want to reach the Elder Triage before nightfall."

"As should we," Eleonora said. "We'd prefer not to be out after dark as well. You wouldn't believe the strange woman I ran into on my way to Faery Kingdom."

"A story for another time!" Isadora interrupted. "We need to go, Nora!"

So Myso and Basil bid the females goodbye and the two groups continued on their separate ways, all a bit weary from their travels and completely unaware of to what was soon to come.

CHAPTER 6

"We're almost there," Basil said, after he and Myso had been separated from the three faeries for quite some time. "I can see the glow of their tree in the distance."

"Ahh, I see it too," Myso replied. "'Tis a shame that the barriers have prevented the witches from putting their home under an invisibility spell. I'm sure that would help defend them."

"It's the times we live in. All that was once invisible can no longer be. The Forest is *forcing* us to see what we previously believed wasn't there."

"Almost like a punishment for generations of ignorance."

"That's what I believe too, my dear friend."

The dim radiance of the Elder Triage's home brightened as the two approached. When they grew closer, Myso noticed that a tree, very close in proximity to the witches' home, looked different than he remembered.

"Hmm, that's strange," he said, pointing it out. "That tree wasn't gangly and black like that the last time we were here."

"It looks like it may have died," Basil replied.

"It looks *beyond* dead, if that makes sense. Look at that dark void in the canopy above. An ordinary dead tree wouldn't have such a thing."

"But why is there a strange black hole protruding from the top of a dead tree?" Basil asked.

"Perhaps that's what killed it in the first place."

The two approached the tree. Myso stopped in front of the tree, taking a moment to study it carefully.

"How curious," he said. "It seems to still be alive."

"Weird," Basil replied, his voice a little shaky. "Perhaps it's best if we move on, Myso."

"All right."

The two scurried away, and soon found themselves at the witches' front door. Myso lifted his fist and lightly rapped on the door three times.

No one answered.

"Hello?" Myso called, knocking again. Still there was no response.

"There's a light on, they must be home," Basil said. "Perhaps they can't hear you."

"*HELLO?!*" Myso yelled at the door, then lost his footing and fell against it, opening the slightly-ajar door and falling face first into the house.

The home looked like it had been ransacked. Lights were on, papers and trinkets were strewn about, and the furniture was completely upended onto the floor. The crystals that once adorned the endless rows of shelves and cascaded from the ceiling looked like they had been torn down and tossed about the room, breaking several of them into tiny, razor-sharp fragments. And, in the very center of the witches' sitting room, was their large crystal ball, smashed into a million pieces and scattered around the overturned, woven copper stand.

"Oh, no," Basil whispered.

"I'm going to check upstairs," Myso said hurriedly. "Maybe someone's still here."

"I'll look around downstairs, then."

Myso carefully crept up the stairs that led to the second floor, trying his best not to let any of the steps creak. When he reached the top, he peered into the first bedroom.

Nothing. Just another haphazard mess, but no living beings.

Myso continued down the hallway and glanced into the second bedroom. There was nothing in there, either, so he made his way to the third and final bedroom. The door was open just a crack. Myso pushed it open.

In the room, several strange beasts sat, perched upon the bedposts as if awaiting Myso's arrival. They resembled humans in a strange sense; though hair covered their entire bodies, their noses were large and flat, and their eyes were as black as obsidian. Upon their backs they each wore a set of enormous, feathery wings that curled around themselves the second that Myso entered the room. As the troll's eyes widened upon realizing what he was looking at, the creatures recoiled into their wings and hissed at him.

"It's a troll," one of them said, his words reverberating through Myso's skull.

"Let's eat him!" another replied, licking its drooling lips over two sharp, elongated fangs.

Myso's eyes frantically scanned the room. There was no sign of the witches that he could see, but then again, he wasn't able to see what was on the other side of the bed.

"Don't eat me," he said. "It's a well-known fact that trolls don't taste good."

"They taste good to us!" one of them declared. "Always have, we've just been unable to eat your kind for many, many generations."

"I know what you are," Myso replied. "And I *know* you are not inherently negative beings! Why are you doing this, reebobs?"

"The humans are bad," the one reebob, who Myso considered to be the one in charge, replied. "They've ruined everything. They've destroyed our Forest. But the Controllers will fix it all. They've returned to save the Forest."

"As far as I know, they're *not* here to help the Forest," Myso explained. "They're here to finish it off!"

"Maybe it's better this way. We can start fresh."

"You do realize that even the Controllers were once human, right?"

"That doesn't matter to us. They no longer are."

"Where are the witches?"

The reebob leader laughed, prompting the rest of the reebobs to join in, filling the whole tree house with eerie, echoing cackles.

"We took care of them, just as we were ordered to. But don't worry, you'll all see them again very soon—in the afterlife."

Myso gulped as he realized that the reebobs were moving in closer, surrounding him so he wouldn't be able to leave the room. He tried to turn to leave, but a reebob hopped off its post and leaped over his back. He no longer had any means of escape.

He unsheathed his blade. "Do not come any closer," he warned.

The reebobs ignored him, curling their wings around each other to enclose him within their trap. Myso slashed his blade in a circle, causing them to leap back. This surprised the troll, because as far as he knew, reebobs had no reason whatsoever to fear the blade. They were immortal; their sole purpose for existence was to guard the vortices of the Forest.

There was no reason for them to be away from their posts, let alone destroy the witches' house.

"Ah, so you mind this blade, then?" Myso taunted, swiping it around again. "If I didn't know any better, I'd say you're suddenly concerned with your mortality. Strange."

The reebobs flinched, causing Myso's eyes to widen in further realization.

"Why did you give up your immortality?" he asked them, not really expecting a response.

"We are still immortal!" was all the reebob leader retorted. "Finish him!"

The reebobs closed in, prompting Myso to swing his blade around once again. "Let me guess," he began, holding his blade ready for another strike. "You've all given up your immortality. But for what, I wonder? The Controllers put you up to it, perhaps? But what could they possibly offer you that would warrant you sacrificing such a key aspect of your existences?"

"Shut your filthy troll mouth," the reebob leader said before turning to the others. *"GET HIM!"*

The reebobs pulled back, then shot forward at Myso, each one letting out a bloodcurdling screech in the process. Myso swung his blade at the reebob attacking his front, but two more from behind him leaped onto his back. He whirled around furiously, trying to shake them off, but they were much larger than him, and a lot stronger, as he quickly found out.

Myso was able to slice through one of the reebob's thin, vein-filled wings. Once his blade made contact, he slid the handle down as hard as he could. The reebob wailed, flapping its now-wounded wing helplessly against its back as half of it hung to the ground in a fleshy clump. Another reebob came out of nowhere and sank its teeth into Myso's forearm. He cried out in agony.

Suddenly, the reebob attacking Myso was pulled backward, and out of the corner of his eye, Myso could see it go flying through the air and slam into a wall, crumpling to the ground in a bone-crunching heap. The sight of this prompted the reebob leader to levitate himself upwards, far too high for anyone, including Myso, to continue an attack.

Two more reebobs flew at the troll, but one was halted mid-air and tossed like a rag doll into the wall, just as the other had been. Myso was able to jab his blade at just the right moment, cutting into the other attacker's lower abdomen. The reebob stopped, placed his hand upon his spurting gash and looked at it. Seeing the blood must have startled him, for he shot up to the ceiling and joined the leader. The two exchanged glances briefly before shaking the other two reebobs awake and pulling them towards the window. The leader opened it, instructed a reebob to assist their broken-winged comrade, and with that, they flew out the window with several high-pitched, ear-splitting screams.

Once their silhouettes were no longer visible on the horizon, Myso turned his attention to the doorway of the room. Just as he expected, Basil was standing there, smiling at his friend as if nothing harrowing had just occurred.

"Need some help?" he joked with a flick of his bushy black-and-white tail.

"Not anymore," Myso replied, grinning from ear to ear as he wrapped a shred of his tunic over the bite mark on his arm. "An odd skunk has already gone and done it. Thank you, my dear friend. You sure seem to have a knack for being in the right place at the right time."

"And you, my dear troll, the exact opposite."

Suddenly, Druzy the bee flew into the room through the window, stopping directly in Myso's eye-line. *"Myso!"* she said, her voice shakier than its normal underlying buzz. *"King Felix is on his way. You two need to stay here until they arrive."*

"They?" Myso asked.

"Yes. King Felix, Kellen, and Narena. And a fox named Earl, with whom they are riding our way as we speak. However, I'm afraid I must head back to Nymph Kingdom, as Felide requested my presence upon completion of this task."

"Then we will wait here for them," Basil replied, as Druzy buzzed out the window and away, into the depth of the Forest once again.

So that's exactly what they did.

Felix, Kellen, and Narena picked themselves up after slamming forcefully into the dirt on the Forest floor of the Earth Realm. Upon arriving where the Elemeportal had taken them, Druzy had flown off in the direction of the Elder Triage's home. Behind them lay Lapis Mountain, about a half-day's travel on foot to the witches' house. With the help of Earl, however, the journey would be much, much shorter.

"Why did it drop us off here?" Felix asked his mother as she helped brush him off. "Couldn't the Elemeportal have taken us anywhere in the Forest, since we are essentially an aspect of the Earth Realm?"

"I'm guessing Lapis Mountain is the heart of the Earth Realm, and that's why we ended up here," Narena replied.

"Let's keep moving, shall we?" Kellen interjected. "Earl, you ready to run?"

"I was born ready," Earl said with a toothy smile. "Hop on, little ones!"

In the distance, several blood-curdling shrieks reverberated over the tree-line, sending chills up and down the little beings' spines. Their eyes shot upwards, and they all were able to catch a glimpse of the reebob silhouettes darting across the skyline.

"Reebobs?!" Felix exclaimed, prompting a groan from Kellen.

"If there's one thing I hate," he said grumpily under his breath, "it's my father being right."

"Then you must feel hate frequently," Narena joked in reply. "Because Felide is often correct."

Kellen remained quiet, but his silence spoke volumes.

Earl sprinted as quickly as he could, his paws pounding hard against the Forest path. The nymph family said nothing more to each other as they traveled to the home of the Elder Triage, but Felix could not help the pressing thoughts that were desperately trying to penetrate his mind. He worried about his beloved wife, Eleonora, and was concerned for his two lifelong friends, Myso and Basil. While he knew deep down that his friends were most likely all right, he couldn't shake a sinking feeling that perhaps Eleonora was not. Whether she was affected emotionally by the presence of her sister, or physically by the happenings in the Forest, however, was still to be determined, and not knowing her status was starting to take a toll on the king's psyche. Normally, he could trust his intuition to know that his loved ones were okay, but at that very moment, he wasn't even taking it into consideration.

After what seemed like an eternity, Felix began to see what looked like some light trails of smoke billowing through the air, coming from the direction of the witches' home. As they grew closer, he realized that although they were indeed approaching the house, the 'smoke' was actually a brewing storm cloud, and a very angry looking one at that.

"We'll have to stay the night with the witches," Kellen said, to which Felix nodded in accord.

Narena scrunched her face at her husband. "Something's not right," she muttered.

Kellen put his arm around her waist. "What do you mean?" he asked.

"I don't know," Narena replied. "My intuition feels as foggy as that cloud up there."

Felix groaned. "I wish I knew where Eleonora was. I'd hate for her to be out when this storm hits."

"Maybe the witches can tell us where she is," Kellen said.

Narena didn't say anything, but found her husband's hand and squeezed it.

"I'm sure everything is fine, honey," he assured, though he barely believed his own words. After a generation of time spent with Narena, he knew all too well that based on her current expression, things were likely not.

The Elder Triage's tree home came into view, as Earl raced towards it with all of his might. He skidded to a halt directly in front of the house, panting as he crouched to the ground to allow the three nymphs to disembark.

Felix had barely lifted his head to view the home when the door burst open, and a troll and skunk came charging out.

"Felix!" Myso cried. "Kellen! Narena!"

"Myso! Basil!" Felix replied. "You're here! I thought you'd be heading back to the kingdom by now. I'm glad we caught you."

"As are we," Myso said. "I'm afraid I have some harrowing news to share with you all before we enter the witches' home, or what's left of it, that is."

Narena gasped. "What do you mean?"

"Well, the witches are not here..."

"And what of Magus?"

"He's also gone."

"The Controllers have them! Where are they?"

"That," Myso replied, "I do not know. But there were reebobs here until we frightened them away. It seemed like they had been living here for awhile, though."

"So there's no way of knowing where the witches are, and how long they've been missing?" Narena said, her voice filled with worry. "Oh, no! Kellen, what are we going to do?" She buried her face in her husband's chest.

"Now, now," Kellen replied soothingly. "I'm sure we can find them." He turned to Myso. "We saw the reebobs flying east. This looks suspicious, if you ask me."

"It was about as suspicious as it gets," Basil chimed in. "The reebobs attacked Myso, and then me when I tried to help him. I thought that the reebobs had one purpose: to guard the vortices. So why would they be acting this way?"

"I have a feeling that the Controllers have something to do with that, too," Narena said. "Just like the disappearance of the Elders. Perhaps we should try to gain more insight by performing a spell inside."

"Good idea, Mother," Felix said, motioning to the rest of the group to go into the house.

When all had entered and the door was shut and locked, the little beings, skunk, and fox gathered on the ornate rug that adorned the witches' sitting room floor.

"I'm going to look for the witches' spell book and supplies," Narena said. "This place is a disaster. I don't even want to think about what may have happened here." Tears filled her eyes. "I'm worried about my friends."

"I'm sure they're fine," Kellen cooed, and followed his wife to help her search.

"I would like to take some time to meditate on the matter," Myso said. "I'll be upstairs if anybody needs me. Tell Narena to come get me for the spell."

Earl and Basil hopped onto a discarded cushion and curled into balls, tucking their heads to their chests. They too, were meditating in their own animal way, so that left Felix standing in the center of the room, alone.

As he waited for his parents to return, Felix tried his best to upright as many items as he could, and generally tidy up as much as his tiny nymph body would allow. But since the witches were in fact human-sized, he quickly found his task much too difficult.

Felix was just about to sit down to wait when Myso came tearing down the stairs.

"The reebobs are coming back!" he cried. Narena and Kellen burst out of one of the downstairs rooms and gathered with the rest of the beings in the sitting room.

"How many?" Felix asked, readying his blade.

"Just two," Myso replied. "But they're headed for the upstairs window. It's only a matter of time before they figure out that we're all here."

"I thought you said you frightened them away," Narena hissed.

"We did, but I'm guessing they have unfinished business to attend to."

The three nymphs and troll stood crouched at the ready, with the skunk and fox poised for attack directly behind them. A loud crash came from upstairs, and several moments later two enormous reebobs fluttered down the stairway.

"I can smell them," one of them growled. "They're down here, I'm sure of it."

"Looking for us?" Felix yelled as forcefully as he could. "Go back to your guard posts, reebobs! You're not welcome here."

"And you are?" rasped one of the creatures.

"More so than you," Narena argued. "You heard the king. Go away and never return here!"

"I know who you are," the reebob replied with a drooling, toothy grin. "You're the little girl who defied Labete."

"I'm not a little girl anymore," was all Narena replied.

"Right, you're a mommy now," the reebob said, nodding in Felix's direction. "We reebobs don't really keep a sense of time, you must understand." He turned to the rest of the group. "Our orders are to eliminate you all. Now."

"Over my dead body," Kellen griped.

"Funny enough," the reebob replied. "That's exactly what we were thinking, too."

The reebob shot towards the group, screeching as one of Kellen's arrows instantly pierced through the thin flesh of one of his wings. Of course, that didn't stop the creature, and he wasted no time hurling Kellen aside as he pursued Narena. Kellen slammed into the back of an upturned velvet sitting chair, but popped right back up, and charged straight for the reebob.

Narena swung her blade through the air as the reebob closed in, managing to slash across his face just as Kellen stabbed him in the spine. The reebob howled, twirling around and around to try to remove the blade from his back. All the while, Kellen continued shooting arrow after arrow into the beast's head, turning the reebob into a hairy, monkey-headed pin cushion.

Out of nowhere, Earl leaped onto the reebob's back and sank his teeth deep into his neck, giving the creature's body a few violent shakes before allowing him to fall limp upon the floor. The beast twitched several times, then ceased to move completely. Kellen crept over to the fallen beast and pulled his blade from his back, wiping it on his tunic and putting it back into its holster.

By now, the other reebob was wholly entwined in a full-blown attack on Felix, Myso, and Basil, but, like his comrade, wasn't faring so well. Felix provided stab after stab into the beast's flesh, while Basil slashed and Myso gashed. The reebob managed to get a few good strikes in, effectively cutting into Basil's tail as it swung around, but it seemed there was a reason reebobs were better off as being peaceful, immortal guardians, rather than vicious predators. True, they were formidable opponents, obviously possessing otherworldly strength and power, but no match for the band of trained, experienced warriors.

The second reebob slumped to the ground, bleeding and teetering on the verge of death. It kept opening and closing its eyes as if unsure of his impending fate, yet inherently knowing what was soon to come.

"More will come once these two do not return to their masters," Kellen said. "We must move on. Now."

"Wait, this one is still alive," Narena said. The second reebob coughed, spurting blood from its eyes and nose, and cringing as if in unbearable pain it had never known before.

Myso drew closer to the beast. "Why did you give up your immortality?" he repeated his unanswered question.

The reebob laughed. "As if we had a choice," it rasped. "All of my kind are controlled now."

"By whom?" Felix said forcefully, yet knowing all too well the answer.

"Who do you think?" the reebob coughed. "We never wanted this."

"The Controllers could not have just done this without help," Narena said quietly. "From what I've read, they've been trapped in their realms for generations. Someone had to have freed them, and they would have needed to build up strength after their abilities were suppressed for so long. This likely would have required the assistance of the Under Spirits, or--" she gulped—"Gorgon."

"Who freed the Controllers?" Kellen demanded of the reebob, crouching down to come face to face with the dying creature. But the beast said nothing, instead letting out one last gasp of air before some more blood spurted, and finally—fell still.

Then it was silent.

CHAPTER 7

Eleonora, her sister, and her niece passed through the gates of Nymph Kingdom just as the moon started rising into the sky. Normally at this time, the guardian nymphs would be securing the borders and lighting the torches upon the lookout point, but as the females drew closer, it was apparent that these supposed "closing duties" had long since been performed.

"What's happening here?" Isadora broke the silence, sounding somewhat annoyed. "I thought Nymph Kingdom was supposed to be the safest kingdom in the Forest."

"Wouldn't it make sense for us to be prepared, then?" Eleonora replied, trying to explain away her own confusion. "Let's find my husband."

They walked over to one of the nymph guards, who seemed more focused on the darkening Forest in front of him than the queen and two faeries approaching.

"Excuse me," Eleonora said, causing the nymph to jump a little bit, as if startled by her presence.

"My queen!" the nymph said, bowing. "Thank god you've returned.

The Forest isn't safe, and it looks like a storm is approaching. You must seek refuge in the palace."

"What are we in fear of?" Eleonora said. "Where is my husband?"

"They are all gone, except for General Felide. Urgent need at the Elder Triage home."

"Thank you, we will go speak with Felide."

Eleonora motioned for Isadora and Dorabella to follow her to the palace.

"What's going on?" Isadora whispered as they walked, a hint of nervousness now apparent in her demeanor. "Should I be concerned for my and my daughter's lives?"

"Maybe," Eleonora replied. "We need to find Felide, though."

Felide was in his son's study, looking over the three-dimensional map of the Forest's kingdoms, a stern expression on his gracefully-aged face.

"Grandfather," Eleonora said softly. "Where is Felix?"

"Eleonora," Felide replied. "I'm glad you're here. Felix, Kellen, and Narena left with a fox to go meet up with Myso and Basil at the Elder Triage house. Something is terribly awry in the Forest again, I'm afraid, and I can't say for sure when—or if—they'll be back anytime soon."

"We just saw Myso and Basil," Isadora broke in, prompting a surprised look from Felide upon noticing that there was anyone else present aside from Eleonora.

"I fear we've entered the time of the reckoning in the Forest, and I do not know enough to say for sure if our kingdom will survive."

"Don't say that," Eleonora said. "Of course our kingdom will survive. We made it through the haunting, we can make it through this reckoning."

"The three of you should barricade yourselves in one of the rooms. You'll be the safest there."

Eleonora scrunched her nose in displeasure. "But I want to help. Let's not forget that before becoming a queen, I was first and foremost a warrior."

"You can help by staying alive. This is a direct order, Your Highness. In times of immense danger, as the general, it is my duty to enact such a demand. In the event of, ahem," Felide coughed and continued reluctantly, "King Felix's demise, the crown must be preserved."

"I guess you really are important," Isadora muttered, though no one acknowledged her words.

"I want to go to Felix. We are stronger together," Eleonora said confidently. "I am no help to the kingdom locked away in some room." She paused. "However, I do think my sister and niece should be protected."

"No, Auntie Nora!" Dorabella cried. "I want to stay with you!"

"I agree with Eleonora," Isadora broke in. "We don't know enough of what's going on. Besides, we're merely citizens of Faery Kingdom. It's important we are kept safe lest the Faery King learn of our demise. The news would be quite disturbing, to say the least." She glared at Felide. "Of course, we are not royalty by any means, but the faeries hold a high level of concern for *all* their kind."

"And their kind alone," Eleonora remarked. Felide let out a small chuckle.

"The Faery King doesn't even know who we are, Mommy," Dorabella said. "And I doubt he ever will."

Isadora snorted, but said nothing in reply.

Felide tried to hide the smile that was creeping over his face, which was very uncommon for him. He knelt down to Dorabella's level, and warmly clasped her tiny hand in his. "I think you're right, little one," was all he said before standing up again and turning back to Eleonora and Isadora. "I'd watch out for her. She seems wise far beyond her years."

Felide had always longed for a daughter, though lately his focus seemed to be more on whether he'd meet any great-grandchildren in the glimmer of time he felt he had left. He was growing older, in looks and demeanor, as the seasons continued to change with each passing sun cycle. And though magical beings—unlike animals and ordinary, non-magical humans—held a slight immortality which rendered them wary only of death by hands of another, most nymphs chose death and reincarnation as a way of furthering their spiritual evolution in a different form, in another life. Magical beings were no strangers to the physical deterioration that came along with age, and often preferred to take their wisdom onward to another spiritual body that could nurture their soul's need for advancement and natural progression, that is, if they didn't perish by blade or arrow on their own.

"I refuse to be hidden away when my kingdom is clearly in peril," Eleonora declared, her normally soft voice now sounding more like Narena's. "How did Felix get to the witches' house, Grandfather? Did he take the Elemeportal?"

Felide said nothing, but his face flushed a deep crimson hue. "Of course not, Eleonora," was all he said, before unconsciously shifting his body to block their view of the area of the bookcase where the Elemeportal lay encased within. "The Elemeportal is broken."

"Yeah, right," Elenora replied. "If you won't help us, Grandfather, then I'm going to find someone who will."

"Good luck with that."

"I won't need your luck," she snapped. "Over my lifetime, I've learned to make my own."

Eleonora stormed out of the room, leaving her sister and niece standing with Felide, mouths agape. Though she resembled a nymph in her current state, all too often the fiery, almost instinctual emotional reactions of her faery nature overtook her. She knew she was being somewhat over-dramatic, but the weight of her current predicament was too overwhelming. She briskly walked outside, and it wasn't until she noticed the blanketing darkness and the looming shadows of the tree branches of the Forest that she finally stopped.

"Oh dear," she whispered to herself, "I've wandered too far." She smacked herself in the arm. "And this is exactly why, Eleonora, you're better suited as a nymph than as a faery."

She turned around and started heading back to the palace. She pondered what she'd do when she returned, all while trying to keep her eyes focused on her destination, so as not to see any hint of reason why her kingdom was so on edge. She'd explain her outburst away and when the moment was right, sneak back into Felix's study and take the Elemeportal to the heart of the Earth Realm, then...

"You're out late for the state of the Forest, now aren't you, little one?"

The cawing voice rang out through the trees, causing the Eleonora to jump. She lifted her chin, and saw two exceptionally large crows, feathers black as night without any hint of the iridescence that would normally reflect a shimmer of the daylight sun. Their eyes, obsidian pools which shone like two buttons from their heads, hinted slightly at interest, but on their own sparkled a genuine mischief that glowed infinitely from within their ocular depths.

"I suppose I could say the same of you," Eleonora retorted, putting her hands on her hips. "Now, if you'll please excuse me." She started to walk away.

"Those magical beings just get weirder and weirder," one of the crows said, loud enough for her to hear. But Eleonora said nothing, and instead continued away from the birds as the other one cackled in reply.

Suddenly, Eleonora stopped. With a purpose, she turned around and marched back to the tree. She stared up, and saw that the crows' attention remained on her.

"I have a proposition for you, crows," she said.

"Oh yeah? Let's hear it. I do love a good show."

"Me too!"

"Okay, okay," Eleonora said. "I'm not sure if you've realized this yet, but I am a queen."

"Uh, huh. And?"

"Queen of the nymphs, to be exact. Now, I can't say how I'll pay you back for this favor right now, but just knowing that I am a queen would theoretically be good enough to know that it will be paid back, in some way, one way or another?"

The crows turned to each other, and one of them said, "Sheesh. You'd think these magical beings would be better at communication. They look just like little humans."

"I know! At least the humans know how to use their language properly."

"I can hear you," Eleonora called upwards. "And that's no way to speak of a royal being, let alone anybody."

"Yeah, yeah," the crow replied. His partner nodded, and craned her neck to look at Eleonora more closely.

"What's this favor, little one?"

Eleonora took a deep breath before asking, "How do you feel about letting beings ride you?"

The two crows burst into loud, raucous laughter.

"Shh!" Eleonora hissed. "The Forest isn't safe!"

The crows stopped snickering. In unison, they drifted from the branch of the tree to the Forest floor, stopping directly in front of little Eleonora.

"Normally, we would laugh at this request," the male crow started.

"You did laugh," Eleonora snapped. "A lot."

"But in your case," he continued. "We're willing to make an exception."

Eleonora scratched her head. She'd never dealt with crows before, and while she'd heard they were extremely intelligent, she'd also heard that they were generally tricksters. At least that's what Narena had told her many times in the past. Narena loved crows, a love that Eleonora never quite understood. And after interacting with these particular two crows, her opinion of them was unwavering.

"Hop on," the female crow said. "I'm Shelley. This is my partner, Emerson."

"Pleasure," Eleonora replied with a somewhat forced smile. "I'm Queen Eleonora of the Nymphs."

"How fancy," Emerson chuckled, as he watched Eleonora try to get the perfect footing to propel herself onto Shelley's back. "Did you need some help, then?"

"No," Eleonora said bluntly. "I can do it on my own."

Eleonora braced her foot on the base of Shelley's tail, grabbed a hold of some sturdy-looking feathers on her back, and with all her might, pulled herself up. She shimmied her way to the nape of the crow's neck, and settled down there.

"Ready?" Shelley asked, cocking her head slightly to the side.

"Ready as I'll ever be," was Eleonora's reply. "To Nymph Palace, if you please!"

"You got it!"

Emerson took off, heading in the direction of Nymph Kingdom. Eleonora clutched tightly to Shelley's neck feathers as the crow lifted gently off the ground, pounding her wings a few good times before spreading them out to soar high above the trees. Eleonora spotted Emerson just a little bit ahead of them, his black silhouette only slightly darker than the bluish-purple sky around him.

After a brief moment of feeling the crisp air blush her cheeks, Eleonora noticed the palace quickly approaching. "That window," she said, pointing to the room she had prepared for her sister. The crows flew in, just as the first drops of rain over the kingdom began to fall.

"Well, well, well," Isadora said before the crows had even landed. "Look who's back."

"I hope you've used the time of my absence to rest, my dear sister," Eleonora replied. "Because here's our ride to the witches' house."

"Witches?" Emerson broke in. "You know they're not there, right?"

"Wait, what?" Eleonora said. "They're not there?"

"Mm hmm. They were taken many nights ago."

"Taken?! Where? And by whom?"

"Some cloaked figures. Other humans, maybe. Or not."

"Other witches?"

"And reebobs."

"I would have followed them!" Dorabella interrupted. She emerged from under a blanket on the bed, scurried across the room and huddled closely to her aunt. "Then we could go save them!"

Isadora clamped her hand over her daughter's mouth. "Now, now, honey," she said. "We don't want to do anything dangerous."

"Well, we don't have much of a choice right now," Eleonora replied. "I mean, you could always stay here with Felide, if you want. You know what? That's probably better. You guys stay here."

Dorabella groaned. "Then why'd you come back in the first place?"

Eleonora was silent for a moment before responding, "I guess I didn't want to be alone."

"We're coming with you," was all Dorabella replied, swinging herself onto Emerson's back effortlessly, which surprised even him. "Come on, Mommy."

Isadora sighed, and watched with wide eyes as her sister climbed onto Shelley's back.

"Izzy?" Eleonora asked. "You coming, or not?"

Isadora took in another deep breath and exhaled loudly before allowing her daughter to help her ascend from Emerson's wing to his back. She sat down haughtily next to Dorabella and folded her arms across her chest.

"All right," she grumbled audibly enough for everyone to hear. "Let's go save some witches, or something."

The crows took flight, out the window and off into the horizon.

CHAPTER 8

It was nearly the break of dawn by the time Eleonora, Isadora, Dorabella, and the two crows reached the home of the Elder Triage. The rays of the blood-red sun permeated through the trees and across the distant horizon, radiating its crimson hue over the Forest's now-looming canopy and drying the land from the overnight storm. It was amazing, and breathtakingly beautiful, yet there was nothing at all comforting about the sight to ease Eleonora's tensions. If anything, the deep color of the morning sky seemed unsettling to her, and all she could focus on was getting her family and new friends into the witches' house and out of the open as quickly as possible.

As they drew even closer to the home, Eleonora spotted an open window on the second floor, so rather than have the crows land upon the ground and enter through the front door, she directed them to fly inside that way instead. The crows happily obliged, and landed in perfect unison upon the bed. Only a brief moment passed before the group noticed the two deceased reebobs lying upon the ground, and Eleonora clearly heard several small, pounding footsteps race up the stairs and into the room.

"I thought it might be you!"

Myso entered the room first, followed by Felix, Kellen, Narena, and finally, Basil and Earl. The male nymphs assisted the female faeries in descending from the crows' backs, and once they'd all greeted each other with warm embraces, Kellen quickly explained why there were dead reebobs in the room before hurriedly motioning for everyone to follow him downstairs.

"It's safer down here," he explained as he practically shoved everybody into one of the rooms and shut the door behind them, making a point to carefully lock it as securely as he could. "We moved the dead reebobs upstairs, since their friends seem to enjoy entering from that upstairs window. Hopefully those bodies will be enough for them to leave us alone during the time we are here."

"Have a seat over there," Narena said, pointing to a pile of meditation cushions that were piled in a corner of the room. "You are all tired, and I'm sure you'd like some time to dry yourselves off. Get some rest while we discuss our next plan of action." She went into the closet and emerged with a large basket filled with food and water droplets, likely collected from the witches' kitchen. "Eat up. You'll need your energy."

Eleonora rummaged through the basket, pulling out a loaf of bread, a smaller basket filled with various types of berries, and another container filled with a medley of nuts and dried fruits. She placed the spread out in front of her sister and niece. Dorabella wasted no time snatching up some of the best-looking food items and scurrying off into the corner, where the four animals had made themselves comfortable.

"Now Dorabella," Isadora started. "You need to share that. This food is for everybody."

Dorabella sighed. "Duh, that's what I'm doing, Mommy!" She looked at each animal with an enormous smile, then set the food down in front of them.

"Thank you, sweetheart," Shelley beamed before plucking a particularly juicy berry from the pile. "It looks great."

"Do you have anything other than this?" Isadora asked, scrunching her nose as she rummaged through the basket. "I'm supposed to be eating a diet of mostly crude protein and greens."

"Sorry, but this is all we have," Narena replied, sounding slightly annoyed by the request.

"If I were you, I'd eat," Eleonora hissed at her sister. "You might not get another chance for awhile."

"To eat?!" Isadora cried with utter disgust.

Eleonora turned her head so her sister wouldn't notice her exaggerated eye roll, but Myso did and returned a slight, sympathetic smile.

"There's no lunch break from saving the Forest," Kellen said. "I know that's a hard concept for you faeries to grasp, but it's as simple as this: either eat now, or be prepared for your stomach to start digesting itself. We don't have time for this kind of nonsense." He glanced at Narena, as if prompting her to say something, but Felix interjected before she had a chance.

"If we keep our eyes peeled, we might be able to find you some more protein-rich food and greens along the way. However," he said, looking at his wife, "it's not a priority for us, so if you want something else, you'll have to search for it yourself."

"Sheesh. I thought you were supposed to be nice and sensitive, Felix," Isadora replied. "But we can't forge our opinions of beings solely on the feelings of others, I suppose."

"Please forgive me," Basil broke in. "But can we focus on the issue at hand here? It just seems juvenile to complain over what kind of food we have when we are fortunate enough to have *any* food in the first place."

"Faeries need to learn gratitude," Kellen snapped in. "This is all too typical of faeries, and that's why I choose not to involve myself in their ridiculousness."

Narena gently clasped her hand into her husband's before saying, "It takes all kinds of beings to make a Forest. While it would be easy to assume that all faeries are ungrateful, we can't forget that our dear little Eleonora has proven to be the exception time and time again. It's silly to say that all faeries are unappreciative just because one has showed herself to be so in a very short period of time."

Isadora huffed and puffed under her breath, but took a few select items from the basket and settled herself onto a cushion next to her daughter. With each bite she took, one would have thought she was eating tree bark, or something equally as unappetizing, but after a few moments of silence she seemed to calm down. Perhaps it was merely hunger that made her so utterly disagreeable at times, but if one were to ask Eleonora, it's likely she would dispute that sentiment entirely.

"Now," Myso spoke through the silence, drawing everyone's attention to him. "What do we plan to do next?"

"I think we need to perform a spell," Narena declared. "To find out where the witches are."

"What about the reebobs?" Felix asked. "What if they return?"

"We'll just have to be prepared for that," Kellen replied. "In the meantime, let's do the spell like Narena said, and hopefully that will shed enough insight to provide us with our next move."

Narena left the room, presumably to gather the supplies needed for the spell. A few moments later she returned, her arms so full that Kellen rushed to her aid and carefully laid out the items upon the ground so

Narena could take a quick inventory of what she had. After a few moments of organizing her supplies, Narena was ready to begin her preparation for the spell.

In the very center of the room, Narena drew a large circle with white chalk, then followed with four ancient Forest symbols to represent the four elements, forming a compass-like shape. Moving clockwise, she delicately placed eight candles around the circumference of the circle, enlisting Kellen's help to set a large, black cauldron in the center. Once it was in place, she sprinkled three handfuls of a mixed medley of herbs she'd gathered from the witches' stock, double checked her setup, and called over the rest of the group.

"Everybody gather within the circle, stand together and hold hands," she ordered. "Or wings, paws, whatever you've got." She gave a warm smile to each of the animals.

The group obliged, and Narena set out in her clockwise motion again, lighting each candle from one of the witches' lanterns before settling in her place in the circle next to her husband. She clasped his rough, strong hand in hers and grabbed Myso's with her other. She took a deep breath.

"Now, close your eyes," she said softly. "Imagine that we are within a circle of golden, protective light. Imagine that light absorbing into your body, seeping into every organ—so the light radiates out of you from within."

Isadora snorted, but Eleonora smacked her in the leg, instantly silencing her. Narena opened one eye and stared at her, continuing only when she was certain that Isadora was quiet. Using a flame taken from the candle pointing north, she set the herbs within the cauldron on fire and watched the pile burn for just a brief moment before wafting the thick, charcoal-gray smoke towards the ceiling, where it bent into a rubbery-looking wave before gliding softly out the cracked window.

"Higher Spirits—we ask for your love, guidance, protection, and direction. Watch over us as we embark on this quest to save our Forest and all our brethren—regardless of species—of the kingdoms within." She paused, taking in another deep breath before continuing. "Arepo—hear our plea! We need your guidance now, more than ever!"

Narena lifted her arms up, prompting the rest of the circle to follow suit. She began her incantation, spoken so quickly and in such a mumbled tone that her words were barely comprehensible to the rest of the group. Suddenly, her body began to involuntarily shudder, and her voice twisted into a pitch that sounded nothing like her own. Kellen tensed, clutching her hand even more tightly, but then Narena's body began to settle back to a more tranquil state. Abruptly, her eyes burst open, rolling back into her head as she spoke:

"The Controllers are back, so my little ones—take heed.
They are here only to cause the Forest to bleed.
Beings, witches, and wizards have become their prey,
The protective barriers no longer stand in their way.

I speak because my existence begins to wane,
I will guide you until the end of my reign.
There is but one way to defeat these foes—
You must go to the places where no Forest being goes.

In each of the realms where they've been kept away,
you will find a crystal to which they MUST obey.
Look for the golden sparkles; they will shimmer like dew.
Fire, Earth, Water, and Air—all four crystals you must accrue.

Once the crystals are retrieved, to Lapis Mountain you'll go,
to pray to us Higher Spirits so our influence will grow.
To the Controllers, then you will take these gems,
Then, my little ones—you'll control them."

Narena gasped, and slumped to the floor just as a slight, barely noticeable wisp of air drifted fluidly from her mouth and dissolved like a puff of smoke into nothingness. She slowly opened her eyes.

"Are you all right, honey?" Kellen asked. Narena blinked several times, having not even noticed that Kellen was now kneeling beside her.

"Don't break the circle!" was all she coughed as she pulled herself back up. "We must complete the spell."

Narena instructed everybody in the group to join her in a brief chant expressing gratitude to the Higher Spirits—especially Arepo—for guiding them. Once that was done, Narena walked clockwise around the circle one more time to blow out each candle.

"So shall it be!" she declared.

Everybody dropped their arms to their sides and looked around at one another. Myso swallowed the lump that was beginning to form in his throat, knowing all too well why it was there.

"Arepo is dying," was all he could muster out. "'End of my reign'? That can only mean one thing, right?"

"But why?" Eleonora lamented.

"It means the Forest is slowly dying," Narena said quietly. "If the Higher Spirits are, that is."

"What about the Under Spirits?" asked Dorabella. "Does that mean they're dying, too?"

"I doubt it," Narena replied. "They're probably gaining more power and strength, if anything."

"This is no good," Basil chimed in. "We'd better get moving, then."

"Good idea," said Felix. "Let's break into four groups, so that we can obtain each crystal faster."

"I don't know about that, son," Kellen interjected, his brow furrowed. "There aren't four groups that I can see where every individual here would be entirely safe. From a warrior's point of view, it would make more sense to form into two very solid groups and have each group collect two of the crystals. That way, we have a balanced blend of warriors and, ahem, those who need protecting." He glared from Isadora to Dorabella, and back again.

"So how would you recommend breaking up our group?"

"I'd have you, Myso, and Eleonora go with Basil and Emerson to the realms of Air and Earth. Narena, Shelley, Earl, and I will go to realms of Water and Fire. That way, we can all meet up at Lapis Mountain when we've obtained all the crystals, since The Controllers and the witches are presumably there." He turned to the two crows. "I hope you don't mind that I've separated you two, I feel as though we may need a set of wings *and* claws in each group."

"Not a problem," Emerson replied.

Shelley nodded. "We want to help however we can. We'll find each other again, I'm sure. Whether it be back at our home or in the afterlife."

"Nothing can keep me away from her," Emerson winked.

"What about us?" interrupted Dorabella. "I thought we needed protecting, or something ridiculous like that. What group are my mom and I in?"

Kellen smiled, but did not even bother to look at her before answering bluntly, "Actually, I've decided that you and your mom are going back to the palace where you'll be kept safe by my father and the rest of the stationed Nymph Army."

Dorabella groaned loudly. "But I want to go!"

"Stuff like this wasn't meant for beings like us," Isadora tried to explain to her daughter. "There's little—if anything—that we could really do to help, anyway."

Eleonora sighed.

"Yep, I guess it's always someone else's problem, right?" Kellen said, unable to hide the annoyance apparent on his ruggedly handsome face. "Not that this stance surprises me in the slightest—you are a faery, after all."

"They're just not cut out for it," Narena whispered to her husband. "I agree with you, they should be kept safe. There's a child involved, after all." She righted herself and raised her voice to say, "We should leave at once, if we hope to reach the palace before nightfall." It was now well into the afternoon.

The nymphs gathered up what was left of the food, secured their weapons on their straps, and headed out the front door. Eleonora and Felix rode Emerson, and Isadora and Dorabella rode Shelley, while Kellen and Narena rode Earl. The troll Myso, though quite substantially larger than a nymph, rode Basil solely keep up with Earl. Knowing that the crows would arrive in Nymph Kingdom before the mammals on foot, the group bid their goodbyes to one another.

For now, anyway.

CHAPTER 9

"You'll never get away with this," Rhoslina hissed. "Our disappearance will be noticed."

"By whom?" Bellis teased, poking a long, pointy stick through the bars of the witches' earth-formed cage. "And by what sized beings?"

"Don't speak to those miscreants!" Elecampane griped.

"Shut up," Bellis snapped back. "I can talk to whomever I please."

"The Yew was right to separate you all from each other," Lorella commented.

Elecampane shot the witch a look that could kill. "I'm sure you old hags reveled in our separation. You know better than anybody that a coven is far more powerful than just one. Just wait until Celandine gets here."

"You know nothing of solitary witches, then. Nessaba was a solitary, and she played a huge role in eliminating those incorrigible ogres from the Forest."

"And look at what happened to her," Elecampane sneered. "And she didn't even fully succeed, as many ogres remain alive to this day, despite popular belief. The ogres are locked away, yes, but not for long."

"Somebody will stop you. The *nymphs* will stop you."

Mullein exchanged a smirk with Bellis. But before Elecampane could blurt a retort, a tall shadow stepped directly in front of the entrance to the cave, blocking the only natural light from entering. The crimson silhouette formed into the hourglass shape of a temptress, complete with sparkling burgundy eyes that seemed to glow. The three siblings looked up simultaneously, and smiles instantly etched across their tired, human faces.

"Celandine," Bellis whispered, her own cerulean eyes twinkling at the familiar sight.

"She's finally here!" Elec cried, rushing to the doorway to embrace his favorite sister. He kissed her cheek before asking, "What took you so long?"

Celandine laughed in her usual eerie pitch, ignoring her brother's question. "I see you've gotten the witches. Nice work."

"Gorgon forbid you'd help us with that," Bellis grumbled. "I forgot how utterly important you were."

"Then it's good I'm back to remind you," Celandine replied, sashaying across the cave and taking her sister into her arms. Elecampane chuckled.

"Where have you been, my sister?" Mullein inquired.

"Here and there. Despite popular belief, I've actually taken care of a few irritants before arriving here. So, you're welcome."

"As in?"

"Let's just say I've set a few 'death traps'."

"Elaborate."

Celandine giggled. Though she was quite beautiful, there was a sense about her that could be more accurately described as unsettling. She spoke unpleasantly slow, and her body floated about like a flickering flame.

As the eldest of the Controllers, she'd always held a sense of power about herself that commanded authority from not just her siblings, but any being or animal who had the utter misfortune of crossing her path. She would answer to no one.

"So you tried the zombie spell, then?" Elec said. "You've been wanting to use that old spell for generations."

"And it worked like a charm," Celandine replied with a wink. "Numerous times, actually—one would have thought I created this spell myself, it worked so well. There are now zombies and possessed reebobs in every part of the Forest, roaming freely and searching for their next meals in the midst of performing my bidding. I spared no one I came across." She paused, as if momentarily deep in thought.

"Well, we are certainly glad you're here," Mullein broke in. "Now that we have the whole of the Elder Triage, we can move on to our next matter... invoking the Under Spirits."

"Oh, goody!" Bellis exclaimed. "Can I have Valerian?"

"*We* are not invoking them, my dear sister."

"Then who is?"

Mullein cocked his head towards the cage that held Magus and the witches. "They are."

"Do you think we should go to the Water Realm first, since we've been there before?" Eleonora said dreamily as she ran her hand over the Elemeportal, her other hand clasped tightly with Felix's. They had arrived just moments before, stopping only briefly in the courtyard to check in with Felide before packing up some necessary items from their bedroom closet. Once they'd finished that—and after a quick moment of romance they wouldn't be allowed for a long while—they immediately headed to Felix's study, where the Elemeportal gave off a strange energy, as if it had been waiting for them.

Now they just had to wait for the rest of the group.

"I think that sounds like an excellent idea, my darling," Felix replied, gazing deeply into Eleonora's eyes.

"Do you think we'll see Sirenia?" Eleonora asked.

"Perhaps."

"Shall I say what is on both of our minds?"

"About the last and only time we went there?"

"And who we were with. It's been ages since we've even mentioned him."

"Garmon?"

Before Eleonora had a chance to continue, the sound of Isadora's voice echoed off the walls, her tone cooing as sweetly as a cat's purr.

"Is that what you're wearing?"

Eleonora turned her attention to the doorway, where her sister came sashaying in the room. Isadora had changed her outfit to that of a world explorer, complete with calf-high boots and beige sun hat. Dorabella scurried in the room behind her mother, a satchel secured to her waistband.

"I thought you two were staying here," was all Eleonora said.

"Nope. We're coming with you," Isadora replied with a grin. "We want in on all your adventures."

"Trust me, almost dying repeatedly while watching it happen to others around you is not an adventure. In fact, there are times where it's a downright nightmare."

"I trust that you'll protect us," Isadora smirked. "And if not, I'm sure Uncle Felix will. Or that big troll."

"*King* Felix has to worry about protecting himself and his wife," Felix chimed in. "But maybe if you snuggle up to Myso, you can earn his protection. He's a much more formidable opponent than I, anyway. With more patience."

"That's debatable!" laughed Eleonora.

"What's going on? Are we ready to go?" Kellen said, walking into the room with Narena, Myso, Basil, and Earl. He glanced briefly at Isadora and Dorabella, eyeballing them up and down with a furrowed brow. "*They're* not coming, right?"

"Well as a matter of fact, we are," Isadora replied calmly. "We want to help."

"You can help by staying alive, and telling that wretched Faery King of yours to…"

"Now, Kellen," Narena broke in. "Maybe they should come. You never know who will end up being the one needed in the heat of the moment…"

"That settles it," Isadora declared. "We're coming."

Kellen grunted, "All right, fine. But carry your own weight."

"You won't have to worry. I'll be with my sister's group."

"Remember Kellen, I'll be accompanying their group," Myso interjected. "I'll keep them safe."

"As will I," Basil chimed in, though it came as a surprise to no one.

"That's a smart idea then, since they insist on going," Kellen said. "And keep an eye on our kid, too, if you don't mind. He is after all, very important. Or so I'm told." He gave Felix a wink.

"Take good care of my baby!" Narena sang to Myso, prompting Felix to turn bright red.

"Mother!" he groaned.

Narena laughed. "It doesn't matter how old you are, sweetheart. You'll *always* be my baby."

Felix pretended to sigh exasperatedly, but smiled as he gave his mother a warm goodbye hug nonetheless. The rest of the group followed suit, embracing each other and wishing them luck on the journeys ahead.

"Okay, let's go, then," Eleonora said finally. "Isadora, Dorabella—come over here." She helped the two faeries climb up onto Emerson's back. Basil walked over and motioned for Felix and Eleonora to sit on his back, clasping one of his claws onto Emerson's spindly leg once they were settled.

"Everybody ready?" Felix called. Everyone nodded in reply, so the Nymph King turned to his queen with a wink of his own, their recent bout of romance still fresh within his mind.

"Okay, sweet-cakes—press it! Water Realm, here we come!"

Eleonora pressed firmly onto the button with an etched symbol of a fish. Instantly, a forceful wind engulfed the beings and animals, pulling them into a vacuum of bright colors and twinkling lights that was all too familiar to the former faery. The very last sight that Eleonora witnessed before disappearing into the void completely was the hopeful, smiling face of her mother-in-law Narena.

Once the first group had vanished entirely from sight and only the bookshelf and Elemeportal remained, Kellen hurried to his group—which consisted of Narena, Shelley, and Earl.

"Are we ready now?" he asked.

"As ready as we'll ever be," Narena replied. "Let's go to the Air Realm!"

Kellen climbed onto Shelley's back and bent down to help his wife do the same. Earl stood beside the crow, taking one of her legs into his paw.

Kellen took a deep breath, then firmly pressed the Elemeportal button with a picture of a bird etched onto it. Much like just moments before, the vortex opened in a swirl of fog and sucked the beings within it.

Before any of the beings even had a chance to process the dimensional shift around them, they were suddenly pulled back, and tossed onto a very dense-looking cloud with a poof of white air.

Kellen pulled himself up, coughing. "Guess the Air Realm was closer than I thought."

"All the realms are close," Narena replied, taking her husband's hand and allowing him to gently pull her to her feet. "But I suppose that would depend on your definition of 'close'."

"Where are we, exactly?" asked Earl. "I mean, obviously we're in the Air Realm, but in regards to Nymph Kingdom."

"Straight up, and slightly across," laughed Shelley. "Emerson and I vacation here occasionally. I sort of know the area. Though I must say, it takes a lot longer to get here if you fly yourself."

"Well, why didn't you say something to begin with?" griped Kellen. "That would've been good to know."

"Shh," Narena said. "We know now." She turned to the female crow and said, "That'll be a big help. Thanks."

"Now let's get to the reason we're even here," Kellen said.

Narena looked around. "I feel like I'm being drawn in this direction." She pointed her finger straight ahead.

"That's good enough for me," Kellen said, giving his wife a warm smile and taking her small, soft hand into his. "Shall we?"

"That's the way to the Sylph Kingdom," Shelley said. "But I don't know if they'll be much help..."

"Why wouldn't they be?" Kellen asked. "They are beings of light, are they not?"

"Is anybody really a 'being of light' nowadays?" Narena chimed in. "Anyway, it doesn't hurt to ask for help. Everything I've read about them says that they are like the 'faeries of the Air Realm'. Aside from their appearance, that is. They look a bit different."

"Faeries?!" Kellen exclaimed. "Now I *know* we can't trust them. How do you know that they're not in on all the dirty dealings of the faeries?"

"Here we go, you and your 'dirty dealings' speech again," Narena groaned. "Honey, there very well may be a 'faery conspiracy' as you always want to say, however..." She gave Shelley a sympathetic eye roll. "*Everyone* should follow the ultimate law of kindness. That transcends all realms."

"The faeries are no longer ones to abide by that law. Trust me, Narena. One day, you'll see that I'm right."

"I hope that day never comes."

"If I am truly right, then so do I."

"So, does that mean we are going to the sylphs, or..." asked a confused Earl.

Kellen sighed. "Yes, I suppose that it does. Shelley, show us the way, if you please."

"Hop on," Shelley replied with a smile. "Earl, I apologize for this in advance."

"Apologize for what?" Earl said, but before he could finish his exclamation, Shelley took off into the air, quickly grasping onto Earl by the scruff of his neck and picking him up off the ground in one fluid swoop, similar to how a mother fox would scoop up her kit. If a fox could fly, that is.

"Sorry!" Shelley called down to him. "Our journey will be much shorter this way!" Earl grumbled under his breath, but tried to make himself as weightless as possible.

The light of the sun waned behind them as Shelley soared over, through, and around an endless array of oddly-shaped clouds. The air was warm and thick, though the crow breezed through it with ease. When a glowing light began to manifest itself slowly in the approaching distance, Shelley cocked her head upwards.

"There it is," was all she said before drawing her attention back to her flight. Just a few brief moments passed before the breathtaking beauty of the Sylph Kingdom crept into view, and by then all the little beings could do was gasp at the sight in utter resplendence.

The palace itself, the focal point of their collective awe, was made entirely from quartz so clear that one could easily mistake it for glass, aside from the striations that shimmered from within. The outside walls were faceted, causing the palace to sparkle in various shades of white and silver. As they drew closer, Narena could see that the palace was adorned with towering columns of selenite, and she noted to her husband that it looked as though one of the towers would be the safest place to land.

"I heard you, and I agree," Shelley called to them. "Everyone—

prepare for landing!"

Narena and Kellen clutched tightly to each other, readying themselves for descent. Suddenly, something appeared to violently slam into the crow's body, forcefully jerking her off course and sending her, along with Earl and the two nymphs, hurtling downwards towards the glimmering fortress beneath them.

Chapter 10

Felix and Eleonora had experienced this before, but that still didn't mean that free-falling from the sky and landing with a hard thud onto the sandy beach was something they relished enough to want to repeat. And yet, there they were again, though this time instead of being accompanied by Garmon, they were joined by Isadora, Myso, Basil, Emerson, and of course, Dorabella.

"Welcome back to the Water Realm," Felix joked to his wife as he helped her to her feet and gave a quick glance around at the scenery. It looked very much the same as it had before—sunflower-colored sand, and varying depths of cerulean blue waves that crashed endlessly onto the shore.

"I would say I've missed it," Eleonora said, brushing the sand off of her legs. "But I haven't."

"What are you talking about?" laughed Dorabella as she scampered in circles around the group. "This is great!"

"Dorabella!" Isadora yelled. "Get back here!"

"Shh!" Myso scolded Isadora. "Let's not draw too much attention to ourselves."

"I don't need advice from a troll," Isadora snapped.

Myso stomped up to Isadora, and got right in her face before snarling, "Listen to me, Princess, and listen to me good. It is my duty to keep you and your daughter safe, true. But it is *first and foremost* my duty to keep King Felix and *Queen Eleonora* safe. Just think about that. Let it absorb into that dense, ignorant faery brain of yours and stew around until it's good and ready to be fully comprehended."

"Her skull might be too thick," Basil chuckled, causing Isadora to shoot him a deadly glare.

"Come on, you guys," Felix piped up. "Let's not forget that this is Eleonora's sister. Even if she is somewhat difficult."

Myso and Basil snorted in unison, exchanging glances as they snickered among themselves.

"Now, let's focus on the help we should be getting," Felix said after a moment of silence. He looked around. "Where do we start?"

"Perhaps we should try to call for Sirenia," Eleonora suggested.

"From the ocean?" snorted Isadora, but everyone ignored her.

"Allow me to do it," Myso volunteered. "I'm to understand there are extremely large fish in the ocean, ones that could easily swallow little beings whole."

"I'm sure they'd choke on you," Basil teased, prompting a laugh from his friend.

"Don't forget—we're on an island," Eleonora said. "Last time we had to have an undine swim us to the mainland."

"Well, then that should be our first order of business, shouldn't it?" Myso replied, carefully approaching the edge of the water as the tide drew itself back to the sea. He stroked his chin as he studied the waves. "Hello?" he called to no one. He turned his body back slightly to peer at his friends.

"I guess she's not there," Felix said. "That means we have to move on to Plan B."

"Is Plan B the same as it was last time?" asked Eleonora.

"Eh, not exactly. Rather than building a raft, this time we are going to utilize our animal friends." He turned to Emerson. "Would you mind flying us across? You may need to make several trips."

"Not a problem," Emerson replied immediately. "Now, who'd like to go first?"

"Darn, I was really hoping to see Sirenia," Eleonora said sadly. "Oh well."

"I'm sure she'd have loved to see you if she knew you were coming," Felix reassured. "Why don't you and I take the last flight? That way, if she does show up, we'll have a chance to say hello."

"Sounds good to me."

"I'll go over first," Myso offered. "Then Basil, then Isadora and Dorabella, then the king and queen. We never know what could be waiting for us on the mainland, so I want to be safe."

"That's an excellent idea, Myso," Felix said.

"All right then," said Emerson. "Myso, hop on!"

Myso obliged and Emerson quickly took off, his reflection rippling on the surface of the clear blue water. Within just a few short moments, he had returned, and took Basil in his claws before flying off again. Once he was back, Isadora and Dorabella took their turn crossing the ocean. Emerson returned as quickly as the first two trips, and Felix and Eleonora were ready, though Eleonora couldn't hide her disappointment any longer.

"I guess she isn't coming," Eleonora lamented. She'd been looking for Sirenia the undine the entire time that Emerson was ferrying the group to the mainland, and it appeared Sirenia was not in the area.

"Perhaps you'll see her again one day," Felix said. "But for now, my dear, we really must go."

"Oh, all right," Eleonora replied, and climbed onto Emerson's back to join her husband.

Eleonora barely had time to scan the water beneath her before Emerson descended to the mainland beach, where Myso, Basil, Isadora, and Dorabella were waiting for them.

"Now what?" Isadora asked.

"The crystal we seek is supposed to be within the Water Realm," Myso said. "And there's only one way to get there."

"And how is that?" Eleonora inquired.

"We have to go in the water, of course."

Isadora groaned, and Dorabella hopped up and down with excitement.

"But what about the fish?" Felix questioned.

"That's the thing," Myso went on. "We need a sea creature of some kind to help us get from the shore to the Undine Kingdom, where I imagine we will either find the crystal itself, or someone who knows where to find it."

"So we may still have a chance to see Sirenia!" Eleonora exclaimed.

"If we're lucky," Felix finished. "We might not have time to go looking for her. We need to get the water crystal first."

"I'll go in the water," Basil volunteered out of nowhere. "I'm actually not too bad of a swimmer, and I'm big enough that the fish should leave me alone."

"If you don't see anyone who can help us, come right back!" Eleonora said. "I'm worried there might be sharks in these waters."

"Keep an eye out for me, then," Basil replied, sauntering down to the water's edge. Without warning, he leaped into a wave, bobbing for just a moment on the surface before completely submerging. It wasn't until he dove down a good few fox tail's lengths below that he opened his eyes.

It took a moment for his eyes to adjust to the water's salinity, but once he was able to see, Basil scanned the dark abyss that seemed to be swarming around him. It looked as though there might be movement to his right, but of course, he couldn't be certain until he got a bit closer...

A trail of bubbles drifted to the surface, so Basil kicked a few times to move to where he believed they were coming from. He swiped his paw around, trying to see what was causing the bubbles, but his terrestrial mammalian lungs needed air, forcing Basil to quickly swim to the surface to take another breath.

Before he could dive down again, a small, brown, furry head popped up right in front of Basil's nose. The face was somewhat similar to his, although adorned with long, thick whiskers and round, beady black eyes.

"Hello," the creature said.

"Hi," Basil replied, not really knowing what else to say.

"We're related, you know," the animal said, giving Basil a smile. "Distantly."

"You don't say."

"What are you doing in the ocean? I thought skunks lived in the Forest."

"My friends and I need to get to Undine Kingdom. Can you help us? You're an otter, right?"

The otter laughed. "Naturally." She dove beneath a wave, then popped up again on Basil's other side. "Why do you want to see the undines?"

"I just need to know where the water crystal is located."

"Ha! I don't know about that. Didn't know there even was a water crystal, but it sounds neat. I wouldn't mind one of those for cracking mussels, actually. Can I borrow it when you're done?"

Basil looked at her as if she'd gone mad. "Uh, no. Not this time. Sorry."

The otter chuckled again. "Oh well. What's your name?"

"Basil. What's yours?"

"Opus."

"That's a pretty name."

"Thanks, my mom gave it to me."

"So Opus, can you help me get to the undines?"

"Sure, but it's not going to be easy. Your friends don't look like they'd do well in the ocean."

"Well, we are all from the Forest, so..."

"It's fine, I think I can still help. Let me get my mate."

Opus turned and quickly swam away, leaving Basil treading water alone. After a moment of waiting, he got nervous about the possibility of sharks, so he rapidly kicked and pawed his way back to shore, dragging himself up onto the sand, panting.

"I... found... an... otter..." he coughed.

"To help us?" Myso asked, but before he could inquire further, Opus and another otter came bounding onto the shore, much more quickly than poor Basil had been able to.

"Okay, we're ready to take you guys. We also got our seal friend to swim alongside us for extra protection. He's waiting in the water." Not too far from shore, a dark snout popped up from the water, and a fin waved frantically though the air. "He's really friendly," Opus went on. "But anyway, this is my mate, Lewis."

"Hi," everyone said in unison. Lewis smiled and waved hello.

"That's Martin," Opus said, motioning to the seal, who was now bobbing closer to the shore. "Lewis and I can take the nymphs, two each on our backs. Martin can carry the troll and skunk... although you--" she motioned to Emerson—"I don't know how *you* are going to get there. You're not, er, well, shall I say... *equipped* to handle the trip to the undines."

"That's fine," Emerson replied. "I'll hover around and keep watch until you return."

"Very good," Felix said. "Now then—shall we?"

"Do something, Shelley!" Kellen cried as the crow continued to tailspin downwards, amidst the echoing screams and wails of Narena and Earl.

"I'm trying!" she yelled back. "My body is frozen! My wings are stiff!"

"Turn your body up!"

"I can't!"

"Then we're going to crash!"

As they fell, Narena began to notice a speck in the distance, growing nearer with every agonizing second that passed. As it came more into view, Narena was able to make out that it was a slender, faery-like figure that appeared to be riding a large bird of prey, likely a hawk.

"Look, Kellen!" she exclaimed, pointing at the figure. "Someone's coming!"

"What do you want from us?!" Kellen hollered. "What are you

trying to do?”

“I could ask you the same question!” the figure yelled back.

“If you let us die, you’ll never know!”

The figure looked as though he was stewing over Kellen’s response. But just a moment later, a poof of shimmering, purplish-gray dust hit Shelley in the side, and she was suddenly able to right herself back to her original course.

“Now,” the figure continued, steering the hawk to fly directly next to Shelley. “You are all still alive, so you can answer my question: What are you doing here? You are Forest beings, are you not?”

“I didn’t know we were forbidden from entering the Air Realm,” Kellen replied grumpily. “But yes, we are Forest beings, and we are here because we seek the air crystal. We need it to vanquish the evil that has infiltrated our Forest, it’s the only way to stop the Controllers.”

“Why is the Forest always so concerned with the Controllers?” the figure said, perhaps rhetorically. “They’re only humans, after all. What harm could they do? We barely even noticed that Elecampane was here for all that time.”

“Well, he *was* locked away...” Kellen muttered.

“But I am sure you are now glad to be rid of him?” Narena broke in.

“I suppose our overall luck has improved.”

“We’re concerned about the Controllers because they want to destroy our Forest!” Kellen interjected. “You didn’t notice Elecampane because he was held captive! We need to know where that was, because it could provide us with a clue to the whereabouts of the crystal!”

“You silly nymphs,” the figure said. “Our king knows all about the crystal, not to mention exactly where it resides. All you had to do was ask, but instead you come barreling in here, just like those darn faeries, thinking that you own the place and have every right to everyone else's property."

"I assure you, we are nothing like the faeries!" Kellen snapped, his annoyance very apparent in the tone of his voice.

"And all Forest beings are *not* inherently bad!" Narena added. "I'm afraid some of our more unfavorable characters have caused your kind to resent all the beings of the Forest. But we are *not* in cahoots with the darkness, I promise you! We need your help. Please!"

The figure took a deep breath as he eyeballed Narena up and down, then stroked his chin, which had just the smallest pointed beard growing from it. "Well, I suppose the least I can do is take you to the king. It *is* my duty."

"Thank you, sir!" Narena gushed. "And if you don't mind my asking, who is your helpful friend, here?" She smiled at the hawk, who looked around awkwardly for a moment before offering a beaked grin in reply.

"Oh, you mean Hemingway? He's my red-tail. Some other sylph warriors have red-shoulders or even peregrines, but we've relied on red-tails for generations because of the treaty we have with their species."

"He's absolutely beautiful," Narena said. "And what is your name, sir? I'm Narena, and this is Kellen, Shelley, and Earl."

"I'm Wilhelm. Follow me."

Hemingway changed course, shooting down toward the largest tower of the palace. Shelley followed suit, trailing behind the hawk as he came to a smooth landing on the large rounded balcony. Wilhem instantly disembarked, allowing Narena to finally get a better look at him.

His energy was that of an older male, though nothing about his appearance reflected any sort of age—or even gender, for that matter—

beyond his beard and hair color. He was tall, lean, and had delicate wispy wings that seemed to shift in iridescence whenever he moved. He was pale, though had striking, deep blue eyes, and silvery long hair that matched his pointed beard. Wilhelm offered his hand to help Narena down from Shelley, but a firm, quickly placed hand upon the small of her back prevented her from accepting. Instead, she allowed Kellen to climb down and waited for his hand to provide the assistance that she wasn't even sure she needed. But alas, once her feet hit the ground, Wilhelm floated through the clear double doors, prompting the group to follow.

"The king is not expecting anyone, so you'll have to allow me to speak with him first," Wilhelm explained, giving Narena a warm smile that almost blinded her with its brightness. "We don't get many visitors to our realm, aside from vacationing birds, that is. We like our solitude, and many generations of peace have shown that solitude does well for us."

"I've been to your realm many times, but I've never entered the palace," Shelley said.

"Yes, that's typical. Please do accept my apologies for stunning you. I had to be sure of your intentions, especially after all that nonsense with the faeries."

"What nonsense do you speak of?" asked Kellen.

"It is not my information to share. Perhaps the king will tell you."

"Then we will ask him."

Wilhelm led the group down a long, glimmering hallway, the tails of his petticoat swishing back and forth as he moved. He turned right, then left, then right again, and finally entered into a room.

"Wait out here," he said, popping his head back out the door before closing it behind him. A few short moments later, he re-emerged.

"The king will see you now," he declared. "Follow me."

Wilhelm strolled back into the room, and as Narena entered she quickly found the interior took her breath away. Much like the outside, varying depths of clear to silver crystals wove through the walls, reflecting different shades of striations that shimmered with iridescent rainbows throughout the entirety of the room. In the very center, in front of an enormous, thickly-paned window, sat a glimmering throne with a well-dressed, lanky sylph seated upon it. So lanky, in fact, that his knees almost blocked his face.

"Wilhelm tells me you seek the air crystal," was all the king said as the group stood in formation, bowing to show their respects.

"That we do," Kellen replied. "We kindly request your assistance in our quest."

"And how do I know you're not going to turn around and hand it over to the faeries?"

Kellen opened his mouth to speak, but no words uttered from his throat. Everyone stood in silence for a moment, before Narena finally spoke.

"I promise you, we will not. We were unaware that the faeries even harbored a similar interest in the air crystal until this very moment."

"But we've had our suspicions about them for awhile," Kellen piped up. "Do you happen to know why the faeries would want your crystal? Because we *need* it—to save our Forest from the Controllers."

"King Lucian would not say."

"Do you think Lucian sought the crystal for the same purpose as us?" questioned Narena.

"That I do not know."

"But you wouldn't give it to them, I'm assuming?" Kellen asked the sylph king.

"I didn't find his intentions to be pure enough," the king replied frankly.

Kellen and Narena exchanged glances.

"What is your name, Your Highness?" Narena inquired.

"I am King Sylvester."

"King Sylvester, my son Felix is the reigning king of the nymphs. He is currently in the Water Realm, seeking the water crystal from the undines, I'm assuming. We are collecting all the crystals in order to stop the Controllers, who are dead set on destroying our Forest, with the help of the Under Spirits. Imagine if your home was in danger. Please, sir. If you give us the crystal, I *promise* that we will do everything in our power to return it."

King Sylvester was silent for a moment, appearing to be deep in thought. Narena shifted her weight from foot to foot, agonizing internally as she waited for his response. She'd never been one overly blessed with the virtue of patience.

Finally, the Sylph King cleared his throat loudly and said, "I've decided to lend you the crystal. I've found your intentions to be pure, purer than that of the Faery King. The air crystal can be found deep in the floating cloud cave, protected by vultures. Wilhem can show you the way, and his presence will ensure that the vultures do you no harm."

Narena gasped in excitement. "Oh, thank you, Sylvester!"

"Thank you," Kellen gushed, bowing his head. Earl and Shelley bowed as well.

"Good luck," Sylvester replied, as Wilhem stepped forward and motioned for the group to follow him. He led them back out to the balcony where they'd landed, and helped the group prepare for their next takeoff. Once Shelley was ready, he hopped onto Hemingway's back.

"Follow me," Wilhelm said, before taking off into the distant sky.

CHAPTER 11

The two otters and seal flew through the water, breezing past a thick kelp forest before diving deeper into an underwater trench. Eels and enormous multi-colored fish peered their large, dark eyes from their crevices, evidently curious about the strange sight that passed before them. Indeed, it was quite odd to say the least, that two nymphs, two faeries, a troll, and a skunk, would be grasping onto the dense fur of two otters and a common seal. Eleonora wished that the sentiment of pure, innocent curiosity would make the undines want to help such an unconventional group of beings.

"Hold on!" Opus shouted before darting into the darkest abyss Eleonora had ever seen. She clutched tightly to the otter's scruff, squeezing her eyes shut as she felt the unmistakable sensation of free-falling. Then, as quickly as it began it was over. She opened her eyes.

The group stood before the entrance to Undine Kingdom, an exquisitely-designed trellis surrounded by a breathtaking orange and purple coral reef as far as the eye could see. Multi-colored fish representing every spectrum of the rainbow dashed from anemone to coral formation, creating a pattern that almost vibrated, seeming to emanate a frequency of song all its own. In the distance, Eleonora could see the iridescent green tails of undines twinkling as they swam around, going about their daily business as gargantuan baleen whales sailed overhead.

"Wow..." was all she could muster, but it came out a gurgle. She turned to look at her sister, whose mouth was agape, likely taken by the sight in a similar fashion. Dorabella looked like she might explode from marveling at the beautiful sight.

"Here," Opus interrupted, handing each being a portable air bubble to place over their heads that she'd retrieved from one of the undine guards. The rare visitor who would be able to make the trip to the kingdom, even those who hailed from the land, was apparently permitted there, and from the looks of it—welcomed. Once everyone had taken in a few deep breaths, they each climbed back onto their marine creature, and the otters and seal took off once again.

Opus led them through the entrance to Undine Kingdom, swerving in and out of the maze that the surrounding coral reef had created. She ducked this way and that way, turning right, then left, until finally she reached the palace, where the king and queen of the undines resided.

If one were to believe that the elegance of the entrance to Undine Kingdom was almost too much to bear, then the actual palace itself would surely cause one to keel over just from the sheer sight of it. Polished gold intertwined around enormously large diamonds and pearls, sunken deeply into place so long ago that there was no way of knowing the exact length of the gems themselves. The palace was clear, and yet sparkled every variation of color imaginable. The undine palace was, quite arguably, the most lavish and breathtaking of any palace that one could find within any realm, and perhaps that's why very few have, and would, ever see it.

"Business in the palace?" a deep voice asked. It was a male undine with wavy, burgundy hair and sea foam green eyes, presumably a palace guard. In his slim hands he held a golden trident.

"Indeed," Opus replied, his voice echoing through his air bubble. "This group of beings requests a visit with the king and queen."

"Follow me," the merman replied, taking off into the palace.

The strange group of animals and magical beings kept close behind him, through what seemed like endless hallways of carved, rock crevices illuminated only by the thick glass windows that lined each corridor. Much like Nymph Palace had looked long ago, crystals of every size, shape, and color twisted across each wall, reflecting beautifully ornate patterns that seemed to pulsate directly in the center of where the beings traveled. Finally, the male undine stopped, floating in front of a doorway and motioned to allow the group to enter.

"Oh my goodness!" a shrill voice cried. "Eleonora, is that you?!"

Eleonora's eyes widened, and she couldn't help the tears that welled in her eyes at the sight of a long lost friend. "Sirenia!"

Sirenia, apparently queen of the undines, swam with such fervor towards the group that the water formed a wave that knocked each and every one of them off of their feet, sending each individual sailing helplessly into a wall. They bounced off, confused, and floated back to where they'd been standing originally. Eleonora, however, along with Felix, were scooped up within Sirenia's soft hands and pressed lovingly against her face.

"I never in my wildest dreams could imagine that I would ever see you two again!" Sirenia exclaimed gleefully before delicately placing the two little beings back on their feet.

"You never mentioned you were the Undine Queen," Felix said.

"Well, you never asked," Sirenia snapped, proving that she was still just as sassy as Eleonora had remembered her to be. "Now, what brings you here today? You must have had quite the journey to even make it here in the first place! Hey… where's your grumpy friend, Garmon?"

"He passed away, unfortunately," Eleonora replied. "It's a very long story."

"From what I hear about your Forest Realm, I think I have an idea of what may have happened."

"What do you mean, Sirenia?" Felix asked.

"Well, it seems pretty normal for beings in your realm to just go crazy and end up killed. Something's wrong over there, it's apparent even from deep within the ocean!"

"You're not wrong," Myso piped up. "Garmon was, sadly, negatively influenced, and like so many others, it ended up costing him his life."

"But life goes on, doesn't it?" the Undine King broke in, prompting all eyes to turn to him. He appeared to be much older than Sirenia, or perhaps female undines maintain their youthful appearance for much of their lives, but either way he looked as though he could be at least twice her age. That didn't mean he wasn't handsome, however, as it was quite the contrary. The hair on his head and face was once dark, though now was peppered with white streaks that swayed back and forth with the movement of the water as his green eyes peered at the group from behind firmly set eyebrows.

"Pardon me," Felix said. "Allow me to introduce everyone. I am Felix, King of the Nymphs, and this is my wife, Eleonora, Queen of the Nymphs. Myso the troll and Basil the skunk are prized members of my multi-species Nymph Army, and we also have Eleonora's sister, Isadora, and niece, Dorabella…" He cleared his throat, "accompanying us on our quest."

"Pleasure," the Undine King replied. "I am King Ovid, and I've heard much about you, King Felix, as well as some of your comrades. Some from my wife, Queen Sirenia, and the rest from the gossip that travels from the other realms."

"It seems as though we are the only kingdom that is oblivious to the events surrounding us."

"But that is not your fault," the king replied. "It is because that knowledge has been purposefully hidden from you."

"But by whom? And why?"

King Ovid chuckled. "Why, just ask your sister-in-law!"

Everyone turned to look at Isadora, who fervently shook her head. "I don't know what you're talking about," she said, her face void of all emotion.

Ovid snorted.

"Perhaps she truly does not know," Eleonora chimed in. "She did leave her kingdom to come live with us, after all."

"There is no way that she could not know," Sirenia said. "It's just not possible."

"Aren't we here for some crystal, or something?" Isadora changed the subject. "How did this suddenly become about me?"

Not that you don't enjoy it, Eleonora thought, and though she felt bad for thinking that, she was proud for keeping it to herself. These were trying times, after all, and they needed to stick together.

"Indeed," Eleonora spoke aloud. "We came here for the water crystal."

"I thought it might be that," Ovid replied. "I figured somebody would come knocking for that crystal once I learned that Bellis had escaped. I suppose you are trying to stop her from whatever evil she's trying to enact now that she's free, and I'm guessing it involves the destruction of your Forest."

"You sure are good!" Myso exclaimed. "Meditate a lot, do you?"

"A king would be foolish not to meditate," Ovid replied frankly. Felix's face flushed.

"Are you collecting *all* the crystals, then?" Sirenia inquired.

"Indeed, we are," Eleonora said. "We're headed back to the Earth Realm after this, to grab the earth crystal and then to meet with the rest of our army. They've been retrieving the air and fire crystals."

"Sylvester will likely comply, though I am not sure about King Augustine..." Ovid paused, trailing off as if deep in thought before continuing, "And you know who keeps the earth crystal, right? The gnomes."

"I did know that, actually," Myso said. "I'm hoping our meeting with King Gregor will be as comfortable as this gathering."

"Gregor is a hoot! Do send him my best regards."

"I shall," Felix said. "Though I've never been one to know the gnomes as being a 'hoot'."

"Get to know them, and you'll be pleasantly surprised," Sirena said.

"If they give you the earth crystal, that is," Ovid interjected. "Gregor might, and Sylvester likely will if he takes to you, but Augustine... him I am not sure of. But then again, he's always been a wild card. Even more so, especially since his kind were all wiped out of your Forest."

"Their souls are even more powerful in their own realm," Basil added quietly, though everyone heard him. "The salamanders are able to best exist in their purest, elemental form in the Fire Realm. In our Forest, they were far too sensitive to the environmental changes."

"Ah, sensitivity. One's biggest ally and yet, the cause of so many beings' downfalls."

"Shall I fetch them the crystal, darling?" Sirenia asked her husband, placing her small, delicate hand ever so softly on his knee and batting the dark eyelashes that surrounded her sparkling, cerulean eyes.

"Yes, my love," the Undine King replied, his face flushed around his speckled beard.

"I will be right back," Sirenia said with a grin before darting out of the room and disappearing down the long hallway. Several moments later, she returned just as vivaciously as she'd left, carrying the water crystal cupped safely within her right hand.

The water crystal was captivating on its own, in wavering shades of blue and green with golden specks glittering from within. It emanated so much of its own energy and vibration that it caused ripples to form around it, coming directly off of the crystal itself. Felix was hesitant to take the crystal from Sirenia at first, but after carefully studying it and giving it a few good pokes, he gently took it into his own hands.

"Myso..." Felix said, but the troll was already two steps ahead of him, holding open his sturdy drawstring bag. Felix gently placed the crystal at the bottom and tightened the ropes, double knotting it just to be safe. The Nymph King tucked the bag securely in his pocket, tying the extra cordage around his belt for even more peace of mind.

"We should be on our way," Eleonora whispered to her husband, who gave an acquiescing grunt in reply. But before the group could even turn to leave, the male undine who had led the group to the throne room rushed frantically through the doorway, waving his arms.

"My King! My King!" he gasped, practically skidding to a halt in front of the undine king and queen. "My King, our kingdom is under attack!"

"Attack!?" Ovid exclaimed. "By whom?"

"Goblin-fish! They seem possessed. Ruthless!"

"They could be here for the water crystal, too!" Myso cried.

Everyone in the group's eyes widened. Isadora and Dorabella's eyes looked like they might pop out of their sockets in fear.

"Send half the troops to help everyone get to the palace safely. The warriors will fight!" The Undine King turned to the group, gripping his trident tightly. "We need to get you out of here. Sirenia and I will take you to the surface, but then you are on your own!"

"We will have assistance at the surface," Felix replied. "Everyone, hold on tight!"

"Follow us!" Sirenia cried, taking off after her husband through a back room. Opus, Lewis, and Martin soared closely behind her, weaving through each room and down the hallways, until the entire group burst through a set of back doors. They immediately began making their way upward—though they would need to pass through what was now a battlefield—in order to reach the passageway they had entered on their way down.

Balls of dark blue fire came swirling from all directions, exploding into the reef and sending debris everywhere. Gruesome-faced, colossally large black and red fish glided rapidly around each eruption, baring their enormous sharp, jagged teeth as panicked undines tried to weave themselves out of harm's way.

"There!" snarled a particularly vicious-looking fish. "*GET THEM!*"

"Quick!" Ovid shouted, pointing to the passageway. "We'll hold them off! Just get to the hole and go straight up!"

"Wait!" Sirenia called. "The vortex you need is on that island I found you guys on that one time! By the gnome-shaped rock!"

"Thank you!" everyone screamed in unison as the otters and seal began their ascent.

Ovid and Sirenia pulled back together, drawing their tridents and pointing them directly at the oncoming goblin-fish.

"Ready, my little starfish?" Ovid said. "One, two, three!"

The tridents began to glow, energy forming on the points. When the trident drew back and looked as though it might burst, a radiant beam of light came shooting off the tips, striking the goblin-fish and destroying them in a blinding flash. Two goblin-fish, however, managed to somehow evade the attack, and continued fervently pursing the group. Ovid and Sirenia turned to help, but were quickly caught up in another advance from the foes, forcing them to fight those fish instead. The others were on their own.

The otters and seal had reached the passageway, shooting themselves upward as quickly as they could, though it didn't seem to be quite fast enough. The goblin-fish were rapidly approaching, their fangs glistening in the waning sunlight that peeked far enough down from the surface. The group was almost there, but the goblin-fish were unrelenting.

One of the fish managed to get close enough to Lewis to chomp down on the very tip of his tail, causing the otter to wail in agony while being pulled a few good fox tail's lengths downward. Isadora, who was riding Lewis with Dorabella, shrieked in a pitch so high it could have gotten the whales' attention.

"Help!" Lewis cried. Opus and Martin immediately turned around and rushed back to his aid. But the goblin-fish took another bite, and this time, Dorabella screamed.

"Stab him!" Eleonora yelled, though her sister looked on in a panic, flailing around and repeatedly calling out for help. *"ISADORA!*

ISADORA, STAB HIM!"

Isadora did nothing, appearing frozen in fear.

Dorabella looked at her aunt, then calmly grabbed her mother's waist. In one swoop, she pulled a long, shiny blade that had been concealed under her tunic, stumbling at the sudden weight of it. With one hand clutched tightly to Lewis's fur, she impulsively swung the blade at the goblin-fish's face with all her might, slicing into its gills. The fish's eyes glazed over, and its body slowly glided downwards, a trail of red drifting behind it. Opus and Martin grabbed Lewis and helped to pull him towards the surface while the other goblin-fish continued its pursuit.

"Almost there!" Opus called, as the light of the setting sun became more and more focused. "Just hold on, everyone!"

Eleonora grasped tightly to Opus's fur as her ears began to pop from the ascent. She could make out a large black form, fluttering desperately just above the surface. The goblin-fish was gaining momentum, but just as it opened its mouth to attempt a bite at Opus, Felix slashed his blade across its mouth, slicing it so wide that the top of its head crunched backwards before halting in its tracks and drifting downwards in the same manner as its comrade.

The otters and seal broke the surface, where Emerson was waiting to help guide the group to the shore of the island. Once everyone had crawled far enough on land, they collapsed together in a heap, taking in the deepest breaths of oxygen that they had ever known.

"I could kiss this earth!" Eleonora exclaimed, prompting chuckles out of the rest of the group.

"We best be on our way," Opus spoke up. "It was wonderful to meet you all. Thanks for the great story. Our pups are going to love it!"

"Thanks for risking your lives for us," Felix beamed.

"Yes, we'll never forget you!" Dorabella said, grabbing Lewis for one last hug.

"Nor will we," Martin chimed in, giving a salute with his fin before jumping back into the ocean, Opus and Lewis close behind.

And then they were gone, and all was quiet, except for the infinite sound of the ocean's crashing waves.

Chapter 12

Narena, Kellen, Earl, and Shelley followed Wilhem and Hemingway across an endless stretch of thick, watery clouds. The further away they ventured from the palace, the more ominous the clouds seemed to become, in an eerie sense that Narena couldn't quite put her tiny finger on.

Finally, Wilhem turned his course, dropping down onto what appeared to be a floating stalactite, immobilized within a dense gray cloud.

"Here we are," the sylph warrior said, just as Hemingway's clawed feet set firmly upon the ground. "Allow me to continue leading, as I suspect the vultures will not take kindly to your presence." He turned to Shelley and Earl. "And unfortunately—animals must stay outside, at the entrance of the cave. We don't want to make the vultures more uneasy."

"Or hungry," Hemingway finished, offering Earl a wink.

"We can do that," Kellen replied. "And I think you'll find that my wife has a way with animals that will not hinder our welcome."

Narena hopped down from Shelley's back and joined her husband's side, taking in the overpowering sight of the cave. Resembling the head of a hooded figure, the earth around the opening only added a sense of foreboding to the dark cave the sylph and nymphs were about to enter. It was frightening, to say the least, but nothing that would cause seasoned warriors like Kellen and Narena to shy away.

Wilhem entered the cave, with the two married nymphs close on his wings. The sylph wasted no time in lighting a torch that was placed on a small lip on the inside of the mouth of the cave.

"Stay close," the sylph warned, before continuing deeper into the darkness. It wasn't too long before Narena started to see a faint light in the distance ahead of her, and before she knew it, they had reached it.

A pedestal, surrounded by lurching vulture forms, stood in the center of a circular room, carved around the inside of the slim cave walls. Atop the pedestal, what appeared to be a shimmering ball of luminescence radiated in all directions.

"Allow me," Wilhelm said, taking careful steps towards the crystal. The vultures simultaneously mobilized, forming a firm, feathered barrier between the pedestal and the sylph. Wilhem cleared his throat before addressing the birds, "I come by order of the king. You are to relinquish the crystal to these nymphs. I assure you, it will be returned. Now, step aside."

The vultures exchanged glances before the largest one spoke. "Another from your realm attempted to steal our crystal. We killed him."

"Whom?" Narena asked, stepping confidently towards the birds. "A nymph?"

The vultures shifted their weights uncomfortably in unison, before the same vulture replied, "It was a faery."

"Do not lump us nymphs with them just because we reside in neighboring kingdoms," Kellen interjected bluntly. "We are *not* like them."

"I was unaware of this," Wilhelm broke in. "Does the king know?"

"No," the vulture leader replied. "Not yet."

"You should have sent one of yours to report on this matter the instant after it occurred," Wilhelm scolded. "I would think you would know that by now."

"It was not too long ago," the vulture replied, his voice void of all emotion. "We can surrender the body to you, if you'd like."

"Perhaps we should take a look at it," Kellen said. "But you may need to store the body until a representative from Faery Kingdom comes to claim it. That could be a long while, since we have much that is required of us before we'll be given the opportunity to inform Lucian of this poor faery's demise."

"The body was not cooperating," the vulture went on, "so we had to put a rock on top of it."

"What do you mean?" Narena asked. "How can a dead body 'not cooperate'?"

"Show them!" the vulture ordered. One of the smaller birds hurried to a darkened corner behind the pedestal, emerging soon afterward with a small, limp corpse hanging from her beak. She dropped it on the ground directly in front of the three beings, where it twitched slightly before appearing to harden where it lay.

"Do we know him?" Narena said, her voice a tad shaky. "I can't look!"

Kellen walked around the body, leaning down to inspect the face. He stood up, turning his back to the corpse before declaring, "No. We don't know him."

"Thank the Yew!" Narena cried. "I don't know why, but I thought it could be my brother."

"I don't blame you for thinking that," Kellen replied. "But we both know that Nyxen is too smart to get entangled in perilous adventures like his sister. At least not anymore."

"I don't know about that," Wilhelm broke in. "From what I gather, the faeries have been acting crazy and power-hungry lately. At least, according to the gossip that manages to make it all the way up to our realm."

"That doesn't surprise me," Kellen said. He turned to the leader of the vultures. "Now, what did you mean when you said this corpse was 'acting strangely'?"

"Exactly what it's doing right now!" the vulture exclaimed.

Kellen whirled around, just in time to see the formerly deceased faery rise up, eyes glazed and unfocused, and turn his head, his gruesome lips widening into a creepy, drooling grin. He rolled his head around his neck, creating a disturbing crackling sound. Then, the dead faery pulled his body upright with a loud crunch, before leaping upwards and practically flying at Kellen, all the while screeching at the top of his lungs like a wild banshee.

Kellen unsheathed his blade, taking a wild swing at the zombie faery. To his relief, he managed to give the corpse a good enough slice across the midsection to cause him to pull away, howling at the sight of his thickened bodily fluids spraying outwards like an unruly geyser. That gave Kellen just enough time to load an arrow into his bow, so when the faery zombie came at him for a second time, he was able to release, shooting the obsidian point directly into the corpse's third eye. The zombie wailed, shaking uncontrollably, but submitted to his demise by convulsing into a puff of dust that crumbled onto the cave floor.

"What was *that!?*" Narena exclaimed, rushing to Kellen and wrapping her arms around him.

"We tried to tell you," the vulture started, but was quickly interrupted by an irritated Wilhelm.

"This is bad, this is really bad," he said, almost as if to himself. "The king must know about this. This is not good. You vultures are supposed to report this kind of thing *immediately!*"

"We were going to, but then you all showed up," the vulture replied defensively. "We had the corpse under control."

"But this is a zombie outbreak," Wilhelm stressed. "It's only a matter of time before the sylph population is affected."

"It was just one, and I killed him," Kellen said calmly. "Not to frighten you more, but there was evidence of this in our Forest Realm as well. Two of our own encountered a zombie nymph recently."

"This is a horrible sign," Wilhelm went on, as if he hadn't even heard Kellen speak. "These Forest folk are bad luck. This is why we never invite them to..." he trailed off until his words meshed into an incomprehensible grumble. "The only thing these wretched nymphs have to offer are beautiful females... not even worth the effort... King Sylvester is *always* right about..."

"We did not mean for this to happen," Narena began, but Wilhelm paid her no mind.

"You must leave," was all he said, in the most curt tone Narena had heard him use since they met. "You must go. You're no longer welcome. Take the crystal and go."

"If you insist," Kellen said, rolling his eyes. "Thanks for the hospitality."

"Give them the crystal," Wilhelm ordered the leader of the vultures, who instantly obliged, handing it to Narena. She cupped it in awe in her tiny hands before securing it safely within her buttoned pocket. The sylph angrily turned to the two nymphs. "Now, get out."

Kellen turned to Narena, who shrugged. "Well, thanks for your help," was all she said before turning in unison with her husband and walking towards the dwindling light of the outside sun.

Celandine etched a complex pattern in the dirt of the cavern floor circling the fire she had just lit in the cave. When she had completed that task, she motioned to her siblings to bring forth the captured members of the Elder Triage.

Mullein, Bellis, and Elecampane dragged Lorella, Rhoslina, and Magus over to the fire and threw them on the ground.

"Sprinkle this powder over their bodies," ordered Celandine, handing Elecampane a drawstring bag. Elec wasted no time in dumping the contents of the bag upon the witches, looking as though he were thoroughly enjoying himself in the process. His enjoyment only furthered when, upon inhaling the pungent dust, Magus burst into an uncontrollable coughing fit.

"Serves you right," Elec grunted, stepping away so Celandine could lurch forward, her arms out wide.

"I call thee," she began, her voice quiet yet purposeful, like a cat's purr. "Under Spirits from below! It is *our* turn now."

"Celandine," Bellis broke in. "Before you begin..."

Celandine sighed exasperatedly. "Bellis, you fool," she whispered. "What is worth interrupting my contact with the Under Spirits? I must know."

"It's just, well," Bellis began, staring in a daze at the hovering, human head-sized ball of clear water that she held within her hand. "I don't know how to say this, Cel, but there's a strange group of Forest beings that are trying to collect all the realm crystals."

Celandine stopped in her tracks, shutting her eyes and exhaling deeply. "I assumed those crystals were already taken care of. But then again, I suppose if you want something done right, you have to do it yourself."

"It's a strange group, Celandine," Bellis repeated. "Made up of mostly little beings. I thought the reebobs had taken care of them, but apparently not."

"You know what to do, then," Celandine said, sounding bored. "Kill them all."

"It seems as though *they've* already killed two of your zombies," Mullein piped up, gazing into Bellis's ball of water. "And they've gotten two of the crystals already by splitting into two groups."

"We need to secure the earth and fire crystals," Bellis said. "Lest they succeed any further."

"They won't," Celandine replied flatly. "Trust me."

"The zombies don't seem to be a match for them," Mullein said. "We must take this matter into our own hands. You know as well as I do what the crystals are capable of..."

"You think I don't know that?" Celandine snapped. "That's why we have reebobs now, remember? To handle these types of incidents and prevent them from advancing further."

"They've killed some of the reebobs, as well," Bellis said. "I think Mullein's right. We need to deal with them ourselves."

"We have more substantial matters to attend to here," Celandine replied. "At least, I do. Elec!"

"Yes, my sister?"

"I trust no other for this task. Send your best minions to dispose of these troublemakers. In the event that they fail..."

"They won't."

"...In the event that they fail, you are to take matters into your own hands."

"But my sister, don't you think that my talents would be best served here, with you?"

"I trust no other to complete this task," Celandine repeated.

"Very well, then," Elecampane grunted, before storming out of the cave.

Celandine exchanged glances with her remaining two siblings. "You both understand why I sent him away, yes?"

"Not really," Bellis replied.

Celandine laughed. "He is the weakest spirit out of the four of us. He will keep our little friends occupied long enough for us to finish what we've started. Then, we can deal with his resurrection, if need be."

"Hopefully not," Mullein added.

"We only need three for *this* spell, anyway."

"You'll never get away with this!" Magus hollered from his spot on the floor, drawing the Controllers' attention to him. His own magic had, during the time since he was captured, enabled him to speak once again, even after Mullein had silenced his voice. The wizard spat on the ground before saying, "Go to the underworld!"

"We'll see you there soon enough," Celandine shot back, kneeling down to his level. "Oh, great wizard," she mocked. "I bet you and your witches enjoyed those long generations—no ogres, no Controllers, pure and harmonious balance in your precious Forest. You must have known that balance would never last—after all, look at your beloved Higher Spirit, Labete. He succumbed to possession, as will all the others, eventually. Gorgon has been displeased with the lack of reverence from his own negative kind, as they—up until now—have *all* failed him. How pathetic that the closest we came to victory thus far was by an insignificant zombie nymph, Rowan. How I wish there were a powerful enough spell to maintain a being's consciousness after a zombie mutation, like how Rowan was able to wreak havoc as one. But then again, I suppose he had been transformed in an entirely different manner than *my* zombies were...

"But it doesn't matter now, because now *I'm* back, and I'm going to make your witches pay for what they did to me and my family. I haven't forgotten the insanity that erupts from isolation, and it certainly hasn't forgotten me."

"You think they are *my* witches?" Magus said with a sarcastic chuckle. "I own *no one*, let alone a woman whose power pales yours by comparison. A woman is never *owned*, you poor excuse for a once-human. A woman is only cherished, and admired for her power. You, of *all* women should know that."

"Nessaba and I were once friends, you know," Celandine replied angrily, seemingly out of the blue. "Not only did she betray me, her supposed 'best friend' even after we had made a blood oath together to increase the ogres' strength for Gorgon. She started the fight with my brothers and sister that drew the Higher Spirits' attentions to our plans, then turned against Gorgon, the very Spirit she swore to revere. She alone was responsible for the demise of practically the entire ogre species. *Gorgon's* ogres! She contributed to this imbalance just as much as I have."

"Nessaba was trying to save the balance! And the only balance we were able to claim from that ordeal came from locking you and your wretched brothers and sister away!"

Celandine gave Magus a swift, forceful kick right in the abdomen, causing the elderly wizard to wince in pain.

"Shut your mouth," she said, flicking her finger across his lips. Magus moved his mouth around, trying to get it to open enough to speak, but found, to his utter frustration, that he could not. Celandine crouched down, putting her hauntingly beautiful face so close to Magus' that he could smell the sweetness of her breath. "It is because of meddling do-gooders like *you* that I spent so many generations kept away from Gorgon. It is because of beings like *you* that the ogres nearly went extinct, and Gorgon lost faith in me and my family. But not for long. The ogres' time has returned, and I couldn't be more pleased that it is I who is given this chance to redeem my coven in Gorgon's favor.

"Now," she said, turning to her brother and sister, who were eagerly awaiting her cue. "Let's begin our spell. Or should I say—our curse."

Chapter 13

"I'm guessing this is our ride," Isadora huffed just as the group turned the corner of a tree trunk. Directly in front of them stood a decrepit tree that, at one point, was assumed to have been alive. At present, it looked more like a stump, decorated with jagged edges that leaped from the base, as if trying desperately to be freed from its foundation. A faint, yet enormous primitive image of a gnome was carved deeply into the wood, barely noticeable unless one were to stop and study the remains of the old tree. Atop it, an invisible, swirling concentration of energy was apparent to all.

"You're not wrong there," Myso muttered under his breath. "But where is the reebob?"

As if on cue, a screeching wail sounded in the distance, growing closer with each passing moment. A small dark figure approached from the mainland, forming the irrefutable shape of a winged primate.

"I guess you've received your answer, my dear friend," Basil commented, prompting a smirk from the troll.

"Prepare yourselves for battle," Felix hissed. "Isadora, I suggest you take Dorabella and hide close by."

"But Mommy, I want to..." Dorabella started, but Isadora hurriedly clapped her hand over her daughter's mouth, dragging her into a thick patch of bushes nearby.

"I see more of them coming," Eleonora pointed out, her voice suddenly more warrior-like. "There are at least three. I anticipate their arrival in three... two... one..."

The high-pitched shrieking came closer, and before Eleonora even had a chance to take in a deep breath, the first reebob landed heavily on the sand with a thud, right in front of the warriors. The reebob's eyes were dark and unforgiving, glazed over as if unaware of its own surroundings. It crouched low, staring down the multi-species army for a brief moment before curling its blackish-purple lips over its teeth in a snarl.

Eleonora gulped, loudly enough for Felix to hear. He softly placed his free hand on the small of her back, giving his wife a gentle pat before pulling back to ready himself. Two more reebobs descended, the sand clouding their forms temporarily, creating menacing silhouettes before the dust was swept away by the coastal wind.

"Any last words?" the main reebob growled.

"We don't want any trouble," Felix began. "We are merely travelers on our way back home. We mean you no harm."

"The vortices are closed," the reebob snapped. "All of them."

"Look, we're just trying to..."

"I thought you nymphs were supposed to be obedient," piped up another reebob.

"And I thought your kind to be gentle shepherds of the vortices. As King of the Nymphs, I demand you allow my group safe passage through your vortex. That's a direct order."

"We don't take orders from nymphs!" the reebob leader said.

"What about from trolls, then?" asked Myso.

"There are but four that we will answer to. Only four."

"I hope you're referring to the Higher Spirits."

"There's only three of those now, you thick-head."

"I know of the four to whom you refer, I simply do not understand why you would give up your own personal power to answer to another."

"Not that we had much say in this, but we are only trying to look out for the future of our species. If you were smarter, you'd do the same."

"Not at the expense of my Forest. Never."

"Then I'm afraid we're going to have to kill you all."

"Then I welcome you to try!"

The reebob lunged forward, prompting his two comrades to follow suit. Felix reacted quickly enough to shoot an arrow at the first. The arrow hit the beast's lower shoulder, just narrowly missing the reebob's heart. It was enough to halt the beast momentarily, but the other two were still coming full-force.

Basil slashed his claws, scraping across a reebob's face and causing the beast to flinch just enough for the skunk to spring fiercely at its throat. The reebob threw all its weight forward, pinning Basil to the ground as he continued to clutch tightly around its neck. Out of nowhere, Myso leaped onto the beast's back and stabbed downwards with tremendous might. The troll barely had time to take another breath before the reebob's body fell limp beneath him, and he hopped off, pulling his skunk friend out from underneath.

"Thank you, my friend! Okay—who's next?!" Basil cried, taking off after the two remaining reebobs, who were having an intense stand-off with Felix, Eleonora, and Emerson.

Myso and Basil skidded behind the rest of the group. Felix and

Eleonora were just barely keeping the two reebobs at bay—sailing arrow after arrow at them, each focusing on a different foe. The reebobs looked quite peculiar indeed, with the ends of numerous arrows poking out of their faces and torsos like chimera monkey pincushions, slapping their hands across their faces and trying to pull out arrows when given the chance. Above them, Emerson soared in a menacing circle, waiting like a patient eagle for his opportunity to strike.

"Wait, wait!" one of the reebobs finally decreed, his face appearing to snap into reality. "Hold fire, and we will allow you passage!"

"You've had enough?" Felix taunted. "Do I have your word on that?"

"As much of our word as we're able to give. We're possessed, you know. Our memories of our true selves come and go with each fleeting wind that blows through the trees! We cannot help ourselves, so please do not kill any more of our kind."

"So, you do not feel your possession now?" Myso asked.

"It will be back, indefinitely. We are all under a spell, a very powerful spell! It hasn't fully taken hold of us reebobs in the neighboring realms yet, but I guarantee you it will soon. I can feel it. I suggest you leave now, lest it return while we are still in your presence."

"And we will not have any more problems with you?" Felix demanded.

"With us, yes. With others of our kind, I cannot promise that." The reebob's face twitched, and its lips seemed to involuntarily curl upwards, as if it were snarling beyond its control. "Go now!"

Eleonora frantically waved her hands to get her sister's attention, prompting Isadora and Dorabella to come hurtling out of the bush, hurriedly climbing onto Basil's back.

"Let's get out of here," Felix said from atop the crow, where he now sat with Eleonora. "Emerson?"

"You got it," Emerson replied, scooping Basil by the midsection with his claws. Though the load was almost too much for the crow to carry, Emerson flapped his wings with enough fervor to lift the entire group up towards the vortex, pulling them all inside. The portal sucked all the little beings within it, swirling them through an endless array of multi-colored lights blinking every which way, hurriedly floating them to their next destination—back to the Earth Realm.

"Next stop—the Fire Realm," Narena said as the group flew away from Sylph Kingdom, courtesy of Shelley. "I must admit, I'm pretty excited at the prospect of possibly seeing Hawthorne."

"Only if we have time," Kellen replied, pausing when he looked at his wife's face. It was apparent that she hadn't appreciated that comment. He continued awkwardly, "We can always come back for a holiday and visit him, once the Forest is back to normal, that is."

"*If* it ever goes back to normal," Shelley remarked. "Now, where am I going?"

"Head west," Narena replied instantly. "We're looking for a vortex that will take us directly to the Fire Realm. There should be one if we just keep going west from the palace."

"How will we know when we've found it?"

"Supposedly there's a permanent cloud formation that will resemble a salamander engulfed in flames."

"Sounds pretty gnarly," Kellen said. "And for how long do we travel west?"

"Calm down, soldier boy," Narena teased, flashing her husband a flirty wink. "We'll get there when we get there."

"Is it a bad time to mention the possibility of a possessed reebob guarding the portal we need?" Earl asked from his place in Shelley's claws.

"Good point," Kellen replied. "We'll need to be ready for a fight, if the need should arise."

"Hopefully it won't," Shelley said. "I'm afraid I'll drop one of you. You all are starting to get quite heavy, if you don't mind my saying so. Terribly sorry, don't mean to complain."

"Not at all!" Narena reassured. "From what I've read, we should be there soon. Granted, I've never traveled in this realm before..."

"Is that it?" Earl called upwards.

Directly ahead of them, a white cloud sparkled as if there were some kind of ethereal mist within it, pulsing as if a flame burned inside. As they grew closer, the shapes of the clouds shifted, forming an unmistakable lizard-like shape. Around it, the outsides of the clouds sharpened, resembling a flickering fire.

"I'd say so," Narena whispered, fully in awe. "It even looks a bit like Hawthorne."

"How can you tell?" Earl yelled. "All salamanders look the same."

Narena smiled to herself before replying sweetly, "You don't know what you're talking about."

"Where's the vortex, then?" Kellen asked.

"We should just be able to fly right into that main cloud, that's the portal."

"All right, here we go!" Shelley exclaimed, before aiming for the cloud.

An invisible force drew the group within the portal, pulling them straight out of the Air Realm and traveling faster than ever seemed possible. The beings barely had a chance to absorb their awe before gravity took over, allowing the weight of the group to hopelessly fall towards what appeared to be an endless pit of fire. Shelley clutched as tightly to Earl as she possibly could, all the while noticing that Narena and Kellen's grips upon her neck feathers had strengthened as well.

"Hold on!" she hollered, prompting the nymphs to squeeze harder. Shelley unlocked her joints, opening her wings as widely as she could and focusing on where she hoped to land. Below her, salamanders scurried about, though she couldn't ascertain whether they were fleeing from her or just going about their daily routines. Though in this time, especially in the Fire Realm, a daily routine was something to be cherished, making it all the more unlikely that anything normal would occur in a realm so afflicted by the state of the Forest.

Shelley released Earl delicately to ground, before landing softly on her spindly legs and crouching slightly to allow the nymphs to disembark. Before they could even brush themselves off after their inter-realm journey, however, a tall, overly large, black and yellow spotted salamander approached them.

"May I inquire as to your business in the Fire Realm?" he asked, brow slightly raised.

"We seek the presence of King Augustine," Narena replied quickly. "And Hawthorne, if you happen to know where he might be."

"I can take you to the king," the salamander said. "But I'm afraid I do not know of Hawthorne's whereabouts on this day."

"Very well," Kellen chimed in. "Take us to Augustine please, if you don't mind."

"Follow me," the salamander replied, beginning to walk off with the group close on his tail. He was surprisingly nimble and quick on his feet, especially given the fact that, like Hawthorne, he walked on his hind legs, rather than slithering on all fours like a typical, everyday salamander. But all salamanders appeared to be walking in this manner within the Fire Realm, so perhaps this particular environment nurtured that form of locomotion, since it was, after all, where their elemental kind thrived.

"And what is your name, sir?" Narena inquired.

"Camus is my name. I'm one of King Augustine's advisers."

"Nice to meet you," Narena beamed. "I'm Narena, this is my husband Kellen, and this is Shelley and Earl."

Camus gave a warm smile upon hearing Narena's name. "I know of you two nymphs. I think Augustine will be glad to have you here."

"That's a relief," Kellen said. "I was to understand he may not take kindly to our visit, since we seek to borrow the fire crystal."

Camus stopped dead in his tracks. He paused for a brief moment, carefully putting his thoughts into words before speaking. "I'm not sure about that," was all he said. "Please, let us continue on our way."

Camus led the group through the Fire Realm, which surprisingly, was not as hot as one would expect, given the fact that magma was nearly as plentiful as the water in the Forest's year-round creek. Igneous rocks of all shapes and sizes formed mountainous walls that enclosed various neighborhoods within the area. In the Fire Realm, varying species of salamanders reigned, their spirits sent back to the place of magical origin once their time in the Earth Realm had ended.

How the Fire Realm differed from the Earth Realm, however, was that the location of the realm was directly upon the entrance to the underworld—if, that is, a being desired to walk there. Most negative entities would prefer to pass through a break in the veil, or by way of magic spell, in order to reach the underworld, for it was much easier than attempting to scoot by the salamanders in their own realm, or even attempt to cross a reebob by traveling through a portal, though that might be more possible now, given the Forest's current state.

"Where's the palace?" Narena inquired, her eyes darting around, looking for Hawthorne.

"Just around here," Camus replied.

The group ducked through a make-shift rock alleyway, and turned a blind corner to collectively witness the breathtaking view of the Salamander Palace. It shimmered in a medley of charcoal tones that ranged from a glossy black to a dusty pewter. Yet the colors were anything but bland, and the textures of once-liquid magma fused with the sharp edges and intricately lined layers of black tourmaline, onyx, and obsidian. The palace was beautiful, but not in the same way as the palace of the sylphs. If the Sylph Palace were to convey a message, it likely would be one of gentle diplomacy, whereas the Salamander Palace decreed fortitude and skepticism. But why wouldn't it? The salamanders were, after all, now extinct within the Forest. It only made sense that they would be wary.

Camus led the group into the palace, up a long bridge that stretched across a seemingly endless, flowing mass of red-orange lava. Sparks flitted upwards, gliding across the thick air before flickering into nothingness. Narena kept close to her husband, walking alongside Earl and Shelley as they all followed Camus through the heavy, metallic double doors.

The inside of the palace was quite different from the outside—a spectrum of fiery colors trickled across the walls, decorated with various sculptures and artwork, likely done long ago by magical, perhaps even ancient, means. Important-looking salamanders of all shapes and sizes scuttled about, but it was one black as night caudatan, adorned with a chestnut-brown stripe that swooped from head to tail, that caught Narena's eye.

"Hawthorne?!" she asked, prompting the salamander to turn around. "Is that you?"

The salamander gasped, clapping his moist hand across his mouth. "Narena?! I cannot believe it!"

"Oh, Hawthorne! It *is* you!" Narena cried, rushing to embrace her old friend. "I thought I'd never see you again!"

"Yes, I felt the same way. I'm so happy to see you! What brings you all the way to my realm? I can't imagine it's been an easy journey to get here."

"We're here on a mission. We're hoping King Augustine will let us borrow the fire crystal."

Hawthorne winced slightly. "I don't know about that, but I may be able to help you sway him in your favor." He seemed to suddenly notice Kellen, and turned to him. "Hello, Kellen! So nice to see you again."

"The pleasure is all mine, old buddy," Kellen beamed, giving Hawthorne a firm handshake. "How's the Fire Realm treating you?"

Hawthorne chuckled. "It could be better. Do I dare ask how the Forest is holding up?"

"Not well," Kellen murmured.

"Yes, unfortunately the Forest is in grave peril once again, and this time I fear it's much worse than the falling—or even the haunting, for that matter," Narena said. She paused for a moment before continuing, "Had I known that visiting you would be a mere portal jump away, I surely would have done it sooner."

"That's the thing," Hawthorne replied. "It is not supposed to be that easy, or else there would be no need for the reebob guards."

Kellen and Narena said nothing, though exchanged glances as they let Hawthorne's comment sink in. It didn't make sense to them, but then again, they currently had a more pressing agenda at hand.

"Shall I take you to the king?" Hawthorne broke in. "Right now would actually be a good time. I believe he's in his study."

"Thank you," Kellen and Narena said in unison.

"I'm Hawthorne," the salamander introduced himself to Earl and Shelley, who both smiled and offered their names in return. "Follow me," he said, heading down one of the many brightly colored hallways. The group hurried behind their amphibious escort, watching his tail curl around each corner he turned. Finally, Hawthorne came to a halt in front of a closed door, and held up his squishy hand, prompting them to wait as he went inside to speak to the king. A moment later, he came back out and motioned for the group to enter.

The Salamander King's study was quite reminiscent of the one in Nymph Palace, minus the large, three-dimensional map that Felix's had. There was no shortage of books, however, and this study had an Elemeportal as well, which was much more prominently displayed than the Nymph King's. An intricately furbished meditation corner took up a good chunk of the room, adorned with a beautifully embellished altar to the Higher Spirits, placed directly in front of a long window that overlooked the kingdom. And, seated upon a round, plush, and slightly damp meditation cushion, was the largest salamander Narena had ever seen.

Presumably King Augustine, the enormous salamander was almost completely jet-black, though his back appeared to be lightly dotted with a few spots of a bright, sunflower-yellow. His skin rolled over his belly in folds, covering his legs like a plump, dewy blanket. Upon noticing the group, the salamander lifted himself up, craning his neck and curling his body around itself to look at them in a somewhat unsettling manner, like a cobra ready to strike.

"Normally I wouldn't accept visitors at a time like this," he said stoically. "But since Hawthorne here is one of my most trusted advisers, I've decided to make an exception just this once."

"Thank you," Narena replied quickly. "It is truly an honor to stand in your presence. I am..."

"I know who you are," the salamander interjected. "And you," he said, nodding at Kellen.

"Then you must know of my wife's lifelong loyalty and concern for your kind," Kellen remarked.

"That I am aware of as well. Even despite the fact that my kind no longer exist in your realm."

"And we are all very sorry for that," Narena broke in. "The entire Forest has suffered from the lack of such a crucial indicator species, not to mention the hole within my heart that formed on the day I lost Hawthorne."

"Hawthorne has been a strong defender for the nymphs, especially when almost all of the other kingdoms have washed their hands of them."

"What is that supposed to mean?" Kellen asked.

"It is rather unfortunate, the way the kingdoms have left your kind out of the politics of our magical world. But alas," he said with a sigh, "that is how it is to be."

"Who's speaking poorly of the nymphs?" Kellen demanded, not intending to sound as forceful as he did. "Is it the faeries?"

"I'm afraid that the consensus among the kingdoms of our world has concluded that nymphs cannot be trusted to re-enact the balance, so the issue has been taken up by the faeries."

"Has anyone considered the fact that perhaps the faeries are the ones who cannot be trusted?" Kellen said. He turned to Hawthorne. "Have we nymphs not proven ourselves to only be looking out for the Forest's best interest?"

"I am but one tiny minnow in an infinite sea of fish," was all Hawthorne replied, not even bothering to look back at Kellen. Instead, he glanced sadly at Narena, who took his hand into hers and gave it a warm squeeze.

"It's not Hawthorne's fault," Narena whispered to her husband, who huffed in reply, but said nothing, so Narena turned back to the king. "Does that mean you've already surrendered the fire crystal to the faeries? Because even the Sylph King would not allow them to borrow the air crystal..."

"Of course not!" the king guffawed. "That whole idea is preposterous, and I will not stand by and assume that the combination of the realm crystals is going to just suddenly stop the Controllers in their tracks! It is simply not plausible!"

"Now, King Augustine," Hawthorne broke in. "We should probably tell them that a faery representative *did* come looking for the crystal..."

"And I sent him away as I should have!"

"Please, King Augustine," Narena said, bending to her knees and lowering her head. "Please, Your Highness, we beg of thee! Lend us the fire crystal and we promise—on our lives—that we will return it!"

The king turned up his nose. "Absolutely not."

"Please, King Augustine," Kellen pleaded in his firm, warrior manner. "We truly need it!"

"I should lock you all up for even asking," snorted the Salamander King. "And frankly, your continued requests are not only boring me, but are downright irritating."

"Now, Augustine," Hawthorne said calmly. "Let's just give them a chance..."

"That's it! I've had enough! Guards!"

Four hefty salamanders slid quickly into the room, each holding a long staff made of singed wood with what appeared to be a flickering ball of crimson fire at the top. They pointed their staffs at the group, sending a flare that encircled them all in a dancing cage of flames, including Hawthorne.

"Get them out of my sight," the Salamander King ordered, prompting the guards to use their staffs to lead the group out of the king's study. The guards shoved the group down a hallway, down a long, winding set of gravel-like steps, and finally, into a metal cell.

"Let us go!" Narena screamed. "We're only trying to help our Forest!"

But the guards said nothing in reply, barely even looking in their direction. The door slammed shut behind them, and the guards marched back up the stairs.

Then it was dark.

CHAPTER 14

"Something is not right," Myso declared as soon as his rear end hit the soft Forest dirt. The rest of the group landed on either side of him, his words prompting worried expressions from even their animal companions. "Something's wrong," he repeated, louder this time. "I'm sure of it."

"What do you mean?" Eleonora inquired. "Should we be concerned?"

"Well, we *should* be concerned anyway," Myso said. "But in this case, I'm feeling strongly that it has to do with our other group of comrades."

"You mean my parents?" Felix broke in. "What are you suggesting, Myso?"

"It was while we were in the portal," Myso explained. "It's just that sinking feeling, there's no other way to describe it. I couldn't get the image of the other group of out my head, like they were locked up in a cage or something. This is purely intuition—I could be wrong. I hope I'm wrong."

"But we know better," Felix added. "It's most likely that you're not wrong."

Myso said nothing, but exchanged a glance with Basil, brows

furrowed.

"So, what does that mean for our group, then?" Isadora asked.

"I'm not really sure," Myso replied.

"Perhaps that we should be extra vigilant about the company we keep," Basil added.

"Very well," Felix said. "Let's head to Gnome Kingdom, then. It should be a little less than half a day's walk from here."

"Why wouldn't they have the portal closer to Gnome Kingdom?" Isadora griped. "Seems silly to go to all that trouble just to..."

"That's just the way it is!" Eleonora snapped, sounding overly irritated all of a sudden. "There's no sense in complaining about everything. You should have stayed at the palace if this is how you were going to act."

"Sheesh," Isadora muttered. "What crawled up your behind?"

"I'm just tired, okay? Plus, I feel a little nauseous."

"Probably from all the portal travel," Basil related.

"Wow, Eleonora, your feet must be swollen," Felix said after studying his wife's posture for a moment. "Maybe we should find a place to rest for a little bit, all this traveling must really be taking a toll on us. It might be hitting you first."

"You have huge bags under your eyes, too," Isadora commented, looking intensely at her sister's face. "If I didn't know any better, I'd say you were..."

"What about the Elder's house?" Myso broke in. "It's not too far out of the way from here, and if it meant we could spend a few hours or possibly even the night resting—well, that sounds pretty good to me, too."

"That's a great idea," Felix said. "Let's do that."

The group headed in the direction of the Elder Triage home, saying virtually nothing to one another as they walked until dusk. By the time night had truly fallen, they had reached the witches' home, and all breathed a sigh of relief once they'd entered the house and locked all necessary doors and windows behind them. They picked the most secure bedroom downstairs and set up camp for the night once they'd replenished their bodies with whatever food and water droplets they could find in the kitchen. Eleonora's head barely hit her pillow before she was fast asleep. But then the eerie dream came to her.

It took place in a kingdom, though Eleonora was unable to decipher exactly which one. She was aware in her dream that Felix and the rest of her immediate group was with her, but she couldn't see anyone quite clearly enough to know for sure. There were others around, though she inherently knew that they weren't part of her group, and they didn't appear to resemble anyone she knew or ever had known in her lifetime.

At one point in her dream, Felix was nowhere to be found. Eleonora knew he was still around, because by some strange sense she could still feel his presence, but despite all her best efforts to search, her husband was missing. It was as if he was everywhere around her, and yet nowhere all at the same time. It was confusing even for a dream, and Eleonora could feel a slight pang of a headache even within her subconscious.

In the midst of all of this, there seemed to be some kind of battle raging all around her. She could hear the clinks of blades upon blades, and arrows whizzing though the air. But the beings in her immediate vicinity were not fighting; instead they looked as though they were merely watching in horror as being after being, animal after animal, dropped heavily to the ground and sunk deeply into the earth, down to some kind of unseen obscurity.

Then, out of nowhere, a gargantuan foot slammed heavily upon the ground, just narrowly avoiding stomping on Eleonora's tiny body. She jolted, trying to move out of its way, but another foot clomped down, then another, then another. Eleonora had nowhere to run to, and she could feel the terror brewing within her, but yet she was unable to avert her eyes, speak, or even scream, so she finally submitted to curling into a fetal position until she heard her name being called in the distance...

"Eleonora?"

Someone familiar was calling her name, but she couldn't see who it was. She thrashed about, whirling her body in all directions.

Where is he? Her thoughts were frantic.

"Eleonora! Wake up!"

"No!" she finally screamed.

"Eleonora, open your eyes!"

Her eyes burst wide open. "Felix?"

"You were having a nightmare. It's just about dawn, Myso and I were thinking it's a good time to leave for Gnome Kingdom." He gently kissed her sweat-dampened cheek.

Eleonora yawned, still shaken from her dream. "All right," she said, offering a kiss in return. "Let me wake my sister up."

"Already been done," Isadora piped up. "I blame the kid here. Little ones have a way of waking up at the earliest possible time. It's fairly dreadful, actually, if you ask me. One day," she said with a wink, "you'll know what I mean."

"Hopefully that will be a day that I no longer value the sanctity of my sleep," Eleonora retorted.

"Who needs sleep?" Dorabella giggled. "When adventure is afoot!"

"You've hardly had much adventure," Felix said sternly. "And trust me, you might not like it when it actually rears its ugly head. But don't worry—it will soon enough."

"I'll be the judge of that, Uncle Felix," Dorabella quipped.

Eleonora and Isadora both snorted in unison, clapping their hands over their mouths to keep from laughing. Even Myso, Basil, and Emerson couldn't hide the smiles creeping across their faces.

"Thanks a lot," Felix mumbled, which only caused them to cackle louder. "You girls are like a bunch of old forest witches."

"If I were a human, I would be!" Eleonora chuckled.

"Very funny. Now—let's head out."

The group gathered themselves and once everyone was ready, they carefully left the home of the Elder Triage. Everyone walked in silence, following Felix as he led them towards Gnome Kingdom. It wasn't too far of a walk, as the kingdom of the gnomes was located right before the darkest part of the Forest. Though once the group arrived, the threshold looked eerily similar to that of the faeries', blocked off by overgrown plants and an invisible energy barrier that was wholly felt by each individual as they grew closer and closer.

"If I didn't know any better," Myso commented, "I would think that the gnomes were opposed to visitors. A mere generation ago, that wasn't the case."

"Everyone is taking extra precautions now," Isadora said. "This kingdom is quite reminiscent of my own."

"Let's see if we can find someone," Felix suggested, leading the group through the thick foliage of ivy, chopping away stems and leaves to clear a path.

As they approached, it started to appear more and more that perhaps no one had traveled in or out of Gnome Kingdom for quite some time. The path bore no footprints, nor disturbed brush, but the group carried on, all secretly hoping that sooner or later someone would make themselves known.

"This is awfully strange," Eleonora said. "Where is everybody?"

The group ducked under a dense trellis of ivy, entering into Gnome Kingdom all at once. Tunnels carved into enormous boulders of the mountainside looked all but abandoned, and no hint of gnome was anywhere to be seen. Mining tools were strewn about haphazardly as if left there in a panic, and even several balls of ore and unpolished crystals were dropped around. Dorabella picked up what looked like a pale, rough amethyst that maintained a citrine-like glimmer to it (likely a hybrid crystal of the two gems combined), turning it over in her hand a few times before delicately dropping it into her pocket.

"Dorabella, put that back!" Isadora scolded. "That belongs to someone."

"Finders keepers," Emerson joked, poking at the shiny part of a quartz with his pointed beak. "I don't blame the affinity for sparkly things."

"If someone asks for that back, you better give it to them," Isadora demanded.

"I will, Mommy," Dorabella replied. "I just feel like I should hold on to this one for now."

"Never ignore your intuition," Myso chimed in, studying a pile of discarded mining tools. "Mine is going haywire right now. Something is definitely wrong here."

"Let's find the palace," Felix said. "Maybe we can find someone there."

"I'm sure King Gregor is being protected somewhere," Eleonora practically whispered.

"I hope so," Basil broke in. "Because it looks like this kingdom may have been under attack."

"But by whom? And why would they go after the gnomes, of all beings?" Felix asked rhetorically. Nobody responded to him.

"I think the palace is over that way," Myso said, pointing to a large structure that appeared to burst dramatically out of the mountain's side. "Let's go check it out."

The group carefully headed towards it, their nerves on edge. Upon reaching the structure, they gathered more tightly together, with Felix and Myso leading the way, the females in the middle, and Basil and Emerson taking up the rear. The palace was quite the sight to absorb, indeed, as it was constructed from only the finest chunks of copper, silver, and ore, mined by the gnomes themselves. A thick layer of moss crept across the entire structure, with every door and window appearing to be generously adorned with thin layers of black tourmaline, a crystal well-known for its properties to dispel evil. All walked in utter silence through the entrance to the palace, and stopped in the foyer.

"Huh," Myso said. "Nobody to be found."

"Where would the king's study be?" Eleonora asked. "And if he's not there, maybe the throne room?"

"Or the dungeon!" Dorabella chimed in, prompting her mother to shush her. Dorabella scowled at Isadora, tearing away from her mother's attempt to hold her hand. Isadora's face flushed, and for a brief moment she looked as though she might cry, but somehow managed to pull herself together enough to simply nod and follow her sister down a long, darkened hallway.

"This room's empty!" Eleonora declared as quietly as she could once she'd peered into a room. "Looks like a study, it has a library and everything."

"No one in the throne room, either," Felix said.

"Healing room is clear, too," Myso added.

"I guess that just leaves the dungeon to check," Dorabella said.

"Well, let's go check it, then," Myso replied to her with a wink before peering down the last remaining hallway. "The question is—where is it? And is there even a dungeon to begin with?"

"There's one in every palace supposedly, even though we went generations without needing them," Felix said. "There has to be one somewhere."

"Maybe the staircase is hidden," Dorabella suggested. "Perhaps there's a spell so we can't find it. Maybe someone doesn't want us to find whatever gnomes might still be here."

"Oh, don't be silly," Isadora harrumphed. "Why would someone go to all that trouble when they could just outright kill them all, or something?"

Dorabella gasped, so Eleonora quickly put her arm around her shoulders. "Don't worry," she assured her niece. "I don't think that's what happened."

"So, if there *is* a spell," Basil broke in, " then how should we go about breaking it? I'm guessing the stairway would be around here." He knocked on an empty wall at the very end of the last hallway that was void of any embellishments. It sounded hollow. "I bet it's here."

"By golly, I bet you're right!" Myso exclaimed, beaming at his friend. "Our next step is figuring out how to make it appear again so we can use it."

"And I'm guessing that if someone went to all that trouble to enact an invisibility spell—especially when other such spells have failed to work in other parts of the Forest—there's something they're trying to hide. We should find out what it is, even if it doesn't lead us to any gnomes. Maybe we'll at least find the earth crystal."

"Well, what do we know about spells, then?" Eleonora said. "I remember Narena telling me about the invisibility spell that the witches used on their house, way back in the time of the falling. Perhaps this spell was similarly cast."

"What does that mean, then?" Isadora asked.

"In the case of the witches' home, my uncle Nyxen was able to speak to the trees, which revealed the hidden dwelling. But most of the tree spirits left during the haunting, so I don't know how that would be relevant now," Felix said.

"There *has* to be something else we can do," Eleonora quipped. She turned to her husband. "Honey, you've been able to tree-whisper in the past. Why not try it again? The gnomes are the most connected to the earth of all the Forest beings, after all."

Felix sighed. "I suppose it's worth a try." He closed his eyes and tried his hardest to concentrate. *Come on, please,* he pleaded within his mind. *Whomever you are, whomever I must ask. Show me the door to the stairwell.*

As if on cue, Felix's head started to pound. "Ow..." he winced, clutching his skull at his temples.

"What's wrong?" Eleonora asked. "Are you all right?"

"My head is throbbing," was all Felix could muster out. Eleonora gently rubbed his back.

"The headache means it's working," she whispered, to which Felix nodded as best he could.

Grandson of Ginia... a voice rang out within Felix's mind. *There is danger in your request. Those who are left of the trees do not recommend you proceed in this quest...*

"But I must," Felix pleaded aloud. "There is no other way."

Very well, then. But take heed, for you are not meant to perish in this way.

"I certainly hope not," Felix snorted. "But thank you, whomever you are. I am deeply indebted to you for your assistance."

"Gnome Kingdom is a lot more in tune with the earth than other kingdoms," Eleonora explained quietly to her sister and niece. "That's probably why the tree spirits were more inclined to speak here."

"Why did they leave?" Dorabella inquired. "I thought the Forest needed *all* their spirits."

"Unfortunately, we're living in troubling times," was all Eleonora replied.

Felix turned to the group. "I think maybe something is supposed to happen?" he said, confused.

Before he could question any further, the energy of the hallway seemed to shift. The air grew thick with a strange electrical impulse, and suddenly, before their very eyes, the wall appeared to vanish into thin air, leaving only a darkened, looming doorway in its midst.

"Well, here we go, then," Felix said, starting into the pure blackness. The rest of the group followed, keeping close to one another.

"I'll stay up here and keep watch again," Emerson volunteered.

"Very good," Felix hissed back. "If we're not back by the time it's dark outside—please come fetch us!"

"You got it," Emerson replied. "Good luck."

The group slowly but surely descended the stairs, trying to keep as quiet as possible. About halfway down, the light began to wane from above, blinding the beings to whatever lurked below.

"Basil," Myso whispered. "Take up the front, since your night vision is far superior to ours."

"All right," Basil replied, carefully making his way around the rest of the group. He continued leading them further down, and once they reached the bottom, he silently motioned to an empty torch off to the side of the bottom of the staircase. Felix pulled a match from his pocket and lit it.

A dingy, moldy smell filled the beings' nostrils. Dilapidated rock formations, dripping with old water were all around them, as far as the eye could see. As they peered around, there appeared to be nobody within sight, though the sense of an additional presence was strong enough that it could not be ignored.

"It doesn't look like anybody is here," Myso mumbled.

"Maybe we were wrong about this place," Isadora broke in, clutching to her daughter's hand tightly. "Come on, let's just go."

"Hang on a second," Felix replied. "I want to be certain that no one is here."

All of a sudden, a screeching wail resounded through the dungeon, echoing off the walls and inciting not only goosebumps, but full-on body chills that sent each being's stomach sinking down into the depths of their guts. Isadora wrapped herself around Dorabella, crouching to the ground to try to make the two as invisible as possible.

Myso, Felix, and Eleonora surrounded the two female faeries and drew their weapons, whirling around in all directions, trying to catch a glimpse of the eerie wailer.

"Show yourself!" Felix demanded. "Only cowards attack from the dark!"

"It is a coward who shall have the advantage, then," a raspy voice hissed back.

"Who are you?" Felix called out. "At least tell us who... or what you are."

The voice let out an unsettling laugh. "Come and see for yourself, little nymph."

Felix took a couple of steps forward, shining the torch into the darkest corner of the dungeon. There, a gruesome figure stood hunched, its back moving up and down as if breathing heavily, drool dripping rhythmically from its agape mouth into a solemnly gray, muddy puddle upon the ground.

"It's a goblin," Felix told the rest of the group. "Just one." He raised up slightly to address the creature directly. "Why are you here all by yourself, goblin?"

"There aren't many of us left, thanks to your kind," the goblin hissed. "So it will give me great pleasure to feast upon your flesh once I've killed each and every one of you. Nymphs taste a lot better than what I have been eating lately."

"I'm afraid you won't be given the opportunity," Felix replied forcefully. "And there is a reason that your kind is no longer plentiful."

"Like the salamanders, right?" the goblin mocked. "All in the name of balance."

"I refuse to let you speak ill of the salamanders in my presence," Felix remarked.

"Do my words offend you? Poor little nymph."

"Tell me where the gnomes are."

The goblin giggled creepily. "Ask nicely."

Eleonora took a step forward, her fingers tapping gently on the handle of her blade. "Please, Mr. Goblin. What happened to the gnomes?

Tell us and we will leave this place and cause you no harm."

"A few of their bodies are here, given to me for sustenance. The rest fled through the hole I am currently guarding. But they can't escape from the cavern in the depths of the mountain to which they fled, so sooner or later—they will all starve to death. I cannot let you through to them. I cannot."

"Who gave gnome bodies to you for food?" Myso interjected.

"The lady of fire. She wants the gnomes kept out of her way. The reebobs helped take care of that."

"How many gnomes survived this lady of fire?" Felix asked.

The goblin laughed again. "Not enough to satisfy you, I'm sure."

Felix reached for his bow, pulling his thickest arrow from the quiver. "I think I've heard enough," he said calmly. Before anyone else had a chance to react, Felix snapped an arrow through the bow, sending it sailing through the stale atmosphere. The goblin quickly tried to move out of its way, but wasn't fast enough to stop the arrow from piercing directly into his third eye, slicing into his skull and splitting through the back of its head. The goblin instantly fell limp to the ground, and Isadora was unable to stop herself from uttering a helpless scream.

"All that talk was just a waste of time," Felix muttered, walking over to the goblin's body and kicking him aside. He peered into the black hole that the goblin had been standing in front of, shining the torch to reveal a long tunnel that looked as though it had been hand-carved many, many generations ago. He sighed loudly, then turned to the rest of the group before declaring, "Come on."

Chapter 15

"Just when I thought this quest was going to be easy," Kellen lamented, his deep voice echoing through the cell of the Salamander Kingdom's dungeon.

"Is any quest ever easy?" Narena remarked. "I think we've just been lucky up until this point."

"I must say, if I were to be locked up with anyone," Hawthorne commented, "I'm glad it's you guys."

"I second that," Narena beamed at her old friend, wrapping her arm around his moist, squishy shoulder.

"Why would your king do this?" Kellen asked. "It just doesn't seem right to lock up beings who are only trying to help their home."

"I wish I knew," Hawthorne replied. "All I know is that Augustine has looked—and seemed—off recently. I'm assuming his main objective is to protect the salamanders and our kingdom, since the extinction in the Forest completely changed our outlook on everything. I just don't understand why he would turn on *me* like this. And completely disrespect my friends."

"Our focus now should be on how we plan on getting out of this,"

Kellen said. "Narena, darling—any ideas?"

Narena turned helplessly to Shelley and Earl, who looked back at her in a similar fashion and shrugged. "I guess I'll meditate on it," she said, sitting down cross-legged on the floor. "Hawthorne? Care to join me?"

"Of course," Hawthorne replied, taking a seat next to her. Almost instantly, a swirl of flames began to creep across his entire body, engulfing him within it before trickling over to Narena and wrapping around her as well.

"Should we try to meditate, too?" Earl asked Kellen.

"I think it would be beneficial," was all Kellen said in reply.

Shelley and Earl made themselves comfortable within a very close proximity to Narena and Hawthorne, settling down and taking deep breaths in unison with the nymph and salamander. A few moments passed before the flames began to dance over in their direction, and it wasn't until the two animals were completely enveloped by the meditative fire that Kellen finally came over, sitting down next to the rest of the group. He sighed, rubbed his palms together, then exhaled deeply, not closing his eyes until he saw the heatless flame begin to slither over his legs and wrap around his torso.

Kellen had not been a meditative child, though his propensity for the activity somewhat increased when he was gifted healing abilities from the Yew during the time of the falling. Still, he was inexperienced in comparison to Hawthorne, or even his wife, Narena. So for Kellen to experience what he was about to, well, suffice to say that it was unexpected was a vast understatement.

Eyes closed and falling into an unconscious state, the mature warrior nymph found himself in a world much different than the one he currently occupied. He seemed to be floating, freely, though simultaneously in complete control of his movements. The atmosphere surrounding him was thick, though not uncomfortable. It was almost warm. Lights flashed in his peripherals, and then suddenly, out of nowhere, a figure was present.

It was the silhouette of a turtle, pure white, with shimmering golden speckles emanating off of his body in a circular pattern. His eyes were closed, and as they slowly began to open, peering back at Kellen with profound, unspoken wisdom, they revealed themselves to be a shade of forest green, twinkling as they reflected the vivid radiance around the figure's body.

"Arepo..." Kellen whispered to himself, though the Higher Spirit certainly heard him, and nodded solemnly. "I know you cannot speak," he continued. "So I fear the only way to communicate with you is by asking yes or no questions."

Arepo shook his head, as furiously as one could describe a turtle's fervency.

"No?" Kellen asked. Arepo nodded, prompting Kellen to think very hard about what the Spirit was trying to convey.

Out of the blue, he heard Narena's voice within his mind. *Fear not.*

Kellen turned his attention back to Arepo. "I shall have no fear?" he said. Arepo nodded. Kellen thought for a moment, then asked, "Are we supposed to stop this reckoning of the Forest?"

Arepo nodded, blinking slowly.

"Can you help us get out of here?"

Kellen was suddenly jolted, as if he were being dragged by the speed of light, hurled into a scene that already appeared to be playing out, as if it were fated to occur whether the participants realized it or not. He saw the members of his group, stacked atop one another, with Earl at the bottom and Hawthorne, the smallest, at the very top. Kellen turned his face to the ceiling, and instantly began mentally kicking himself for not having noticed it before. The bars of the cage that the group was within did not extend fully to the ceiling. There was just enough space for a tiny, skinny being—perhaps the size of a salamander no longer fully held captive by the burden of a Forest Realm extant body—to fit through. Of course, once the said being *did* slide through, there was one way and one way only to get to the keys that hung at the side of the dungeon door—a long drop. Hopefully whomever enacted this plan would be physically sound enough to manage that fall, and as Kellen observed the scene he wondered more and more if there was any possibility that he himself could fit through the opening. As he studied it further, he determined that for the sake of Hawthorne's safety in his own realm, it *should* be him to do it.

"Eureka!" he declared, coming out of his meditative state more forcefully and quickly than he probably should have. It must have surprised his comrades, indeed, for the rest of the group jolted awake promptly at the sound of his voice.

"What is it, my love?" Narena asked, placing her hand on her husband's waist. "What did you see?"

"Look up," was all Kellen replied with a smirk. The group simultaneously turned their eyes upwards and smiles of realization stretched across their faces before they all looked back to Kellen.

"Are you thinking what I'm thinking?" Shelley said with a beaked grin. "It's a shame this cell is too small for me to just fly you up, but my wingspan is far too wide."

"Already on it," Earl chimed in, lowering his body to allow Shelley to delicately step onto his back.

"Should we have Hawthorne climb through the top, since he's the smallest?" Narena inquired, as Hawthorne watched on with big, beady eyes.

"I really think I should be the one to do it," Kellen replied hurriedly. "My vision indicated that Hawthorne could get hurt, since he's quite a bit older than us."

"But his strength and abilities—even his lifespan—are wholly different than they were in our Forest Realm," Narena tried to explain. "And remember how I was telling you that sometimes certain souls of beings needed to come to our realm to teach the Forest beings lessons about..."

"Yeah, yeah, honey. I remember. But you just need to trust me on this one."

"Of course I trust you, Kellen, but I just have a bad feeling about..."

"Honey. I've got this one. Okay?"

Narena lowered her eyes, pursing her lips tightly. "Very well." She exchanged a worried glance with Hawthorne.

"Will you guys cool it?" Kellen said, helping his wife and Hawthorne climb onto Shelley's back. "I've got this," he repeated. "All your worries are making me unnecessarily nervous."

"Sorry, dear," Narena said. "I'm sending you the utmost light and love."

"I'll be fine," Kellen said, hoisting himself onto Shelley before peering down at Earl. "Ready, Earl? On the count of three, both you and Shelley stand up. Narena and Hawthorne, I'm going to step into your hands and everybody is going to toss me up. I'll grab onto the top of the rail, swing myself over, and drop safely to the ground. Got it?"

"Got it," everyone replied in unison.

"Okay, here we go. One... two... three!"

Kellen felt himself abruptly become weightless, and for a brief instant he felt as though he was a bird, like Shelley, soaring through the sky. When he saw the bar at the top of the cell, he grabbed it, his muscles clenching as he grasped tightly before pulling his whole body up. He swung one leg over, and then the other, readying himself for his drop.

Don't look, and don't be afraid, he thought, but he couldn't help just one, quick glance at the hard stone floor below. Then he let go.

Something cracked, and something else crunched, but before he knew it, Kellen was lying on the ground in front of the cell door, crumpled in a heap. Narena clapped her hand over her mouth to keep from screaming, while the rest of the group collectively gasped.

"Kellen! Kellen, you're hurt!" Hawthorne exclaimed.

"He's going to need to heal himself," Narena choked out between sobs. "Kellen, put your hands over..."

"I'm only able to heal others," Kellen squeaked through his immense pain. He wasn't sure if just one of his legs was broken, or both, but he did know that he could no longer feel much below his waistline. He cringed furiously, angry at himself for making such a stupid mistake. He shouldn't have let his pride get in the way—he should have let Hawthorne be the one to climb over the top.

"He's right," Hawthorne said sadly. "It's a blessing and a curse, as if an almost laughable balance. Those who are gifted with the abilities to heal others may do so at the expense to themselves."

"Can't you heal him, Hawthorne?" Narena begged. "Please?" But she knew that he couldn't. If he were able to, so would she, for she inherited Hawthorne's sage abilities when he passed from the Forest Realm. And though being a sage had benefited her in many other ways throughout her lifetime, healing was not something she could inherently master, like Kellen's powers bestowed upon him by the Highest Spirit.

"Our only hope would be to get him back to Nymph Palace," Hawthorne explained. "He can't continue on with us this way, he'd surely," he gulped before continuing, "perish."

Narena gasped, tears streaming down her face. "We have to get you home, Kellen."

Kellen sighed, a sigh Narena had never once heard in all her time spent with her warrior husband, even when they were kids. It was a sigh of surrender, something that Kellen had never once, ever, been inclined to do. His sigh was acquiescence of defeat, but he did want to at least attempt to make one more contribution before he completely gave up for the sake of his health, well-being, and well—life.

"At least let me get you guys out of there," he grumbled, pulling himself with all his upper-body strength. He very painfully dragged himself across the floor, slowly but surely up the jagged staircase to where the keys hung. He plucked them from the wall and dropped them into his pocket before allowing his body to delicately (though not without agony) slide himself by his rear end back down to the bottom of the stairs. He tossed the keys through the bars of the cage, and Narena quickly snatched them up, unlocking the door and rushing out to weep into her husband's chest.

"Shelley is going to fly you back to Nymph Kingdom," she said.

Kellen shook his head. "No, I think you need Shelley. Let's get the fire crystal, then we'll take a portal back to the Earth Realm. Once we're there, I'll figure out a way to get home."

"I'll be taking you, then," piped up Earl. "It would truly be an honor."

Kellen smiled before replying with a deep exhale, "All right."

"Actually, I think you and Earl should leave immediately, for your own safety," Hawthorne said hurriedly. "I'd hate for you to be injured or," he gulped, "worse if they find you two waiting here for us. After how Augustine just treated me, I'm not sure if I trust his judgment anymore. And anyway, I know where Augustine keeps the fire crystal. Narena and I can sneak over there and take it." He placed his hand gently on Kellen's shoulder, giving him a sympathetic pat. "The portal to the Earth Realm is located just a short distance west from the portal you entered from. You'll recognize it by the gnome-shaped igneous rock. Simply stand tall upon the rock and the portal should suck you straight within it."

"Thank you, Hawthorne," Kellen said. "I apologize for my ignorance. I wish you all the very best of luck."

"You're very welcome," Hawthorne replied before turning to Narena. "Are you ready? Let's go."

"Not before our goodbyes!" Narena cried, wrapping her arms around her fallen husband. "We never leave each other without a proper goodbye."

Chapter 16

The tunnel was damp, smelled of moldy fruit and stale air, and worst of all—seemed to have no end. Felix and the rest of the group walked for what felt like ages, though Felix and Eleonora were not unaccustomed to traveling aimlessly through a darkened pathway.

"Can you see anything, Basil?" the Nymph King asked, trying to squint as far ahead of himself as he could. Their torch was waning—probably due to lack of oxygen—and only one fox tail's length ahead of him was visible to those who were not blessed with night vision like the skunk.

"It looks like there's a very faint light up ahead," Basil said. "You guys should be able to see it pretty soon."

The group kept moving, this time more quickly than before, until finally a light began to just barely twinkle in the distance, almost like a faraway lighthouse in the midst of a terrible storm. As they grew closer, the light intensified, and before they knew it, they were able to ascertain exactly where the light was radiating from.

"It's a lantern," Myso whispered, leaning down slightly to take a closer look.

"Perhaps it's leading somewhere," Felix remarked. "Are there more up ahead, Basil?"

Basil squinted further into the darkness beyond where the group stood. "No, it doesn't look like it."

"Then why would it just randomly be left here?" Eleonora inquired.

"Maybe to indicate that we should keep going?" Isadora suggested.

"What if it's a marker for something?" Dorabella broke in.

"That's a good point," Myso replied, beaming at the little faery. "We should be certain that it's not some kind of marker before we move on."

"How will we know if it is or not?" Isadora asked.

Everyone turned to Felix. It was silent for a moment before he finally said, "Well, shall I see if the tree spirits can hear me all the way down here?"

"It's worth a shot," Eleonora said. "What's the harm in trying?"

Felix closed his eyes and attempted to concentrate, silently asking for the tree spirits to make themselves known once again. This time, try as he might, no headache came, nor did any voices. There was only pure silence, a quiet that Felix was all too familiar with.

"Nothing's happening," he said glumly. "We must be too far underground for the tree spirits to hear."

"What if we messed with the lantern a little bit?" Dorabella suggested, her voice barely an audible squeak.

"I'm not sure if we should even touch it," Isadora remarked. "What if it's cursed or something?"

"We could only be so lucky to be cursed at this point," joked Myso. "If no one else will try, I'm game to poke at it. Couldn't hurt, right?" He beamed at Dorabella, who smiled back at the troll.

Myso approached the lantern carefully, kicking it slightly with his foot before drawing in closer. The light within flickered, almost as if laughing at his feeble attempt, and quickly returned to burning steadily. Myso leaned down, carefully opening the tiny door that led to the fire within.

"Hello little fire," he whispered so softly that nobody heard except for Basil's sensitive ears. "Have we completely lost our way?"

The fire seemed to dance, bouncing up and down as if coercing the troll to continue. So he did.

"If we keep walking this way," he said, pointing to the path ahead of them. "Will we reach the gnomes' hiding place?"

The flame shot up towards the very top of the lantern, practically singeing Myso's face in the process and causing him to leap backwards.

"I'm guessing that's a yes," Basil muttered. "It almost reminds me of a pendulum, in the way it responds to yes or no questions."

"Huh," Myso replied. "I think you're right, Basil." He leaned close to the lantern once more before asking, "Is there danger up ahead?"

The flame jumped up once again.

"I'd say that's a yes," Felix commented. "We should be extra careful as we continue on."

"I'm still confused as to why this is even here," Eleonora broke in. "It wouldn't make much sense to provide a divination tool when a goblin or such could very well use it."

"Perhaps the magic only works for certain species," Basil said. "Maybe the goblins aren't capable of using it to their advantage."

"You're probably right," Myso replied. "Goblins certainly aren't known for their brain capacity."

"Well, then we should probably keep going," Felix said, continuing down the path. By now, the torch was almost completely out, so the group followed closely behind Basil as they ventured further into the darkness.

Muffled sounds became audible as the waning light in the distance grew ever so brighter. As the group approached, the mumbling became louder, until finally it stopped just before they turned a corner. A hollowed-out cavern, illuminated by what appeared to be more enchanted lanterns, was adorned with shelves upon shelves of small skeletons. The uppermost shelves displayed rows and rows of ancient gnome skulls, with the lower shelves holding the remainder of the bones. The mere sight of it was enough to collectively take each individual's breath away, and all were aware that this was not only the final resting place for dozens of the Forest's original gnome inhabitants, but of an energy that could only come from the sanctity of a deeply holy place. Whether the barely audible whispers that echoed through the chamber were heard by the members of the group or not, they were certainly present.

"It's some kind of gnome catacomb," Myso commented.

"And look!" Eleonora exclaimed. "It appears that several beings are living here."

"Or trying to, anyway," Felix finished. His eyes scanned as best they could in the dim lighting, stopping on an object upon one of the shelves, next to a skull, that twinkled as he shifted his weight from foot to foot. "Hey!" he cried, pointing upwards. "I think that might be the earth crystal up there!"

All faces turned simultaneously, eyes widening as they all came to the same conclusion.

"But how are we going to get it?" Isadora asked. "It's up pretty high."

"Hey, remember that being-ladder that everyone made in order to save us from the underworld, honey?" Eleonora said. "What if we tried doing something like that?"

"That's not a bad idea," Felix replied.

"But what do we do if the gnomes come back?" Isadora said.

"And how did they manage to leave in the first place?" Dorabella continued. "They couldn't have left the way we came, or we'd have run into them, right?"

"I'd agree with that," Myso said. "There has to be another exit that we are not seeing."

"Let's just grab the crystal and go," Felix interjected. "We don't know how long it's been since we got here, and my parents are probably waiting for us at Lapis Mountain by now."

"We should at least find out what happened to the gnomes," Eleonora said. "And ask them if it's okay to even take the earth crystal."

"We're planning on returning it," Felix snapped, prompting a death glare from his wife. His demeanor instantly softened before he continued. "But I suppose it couldn't hurt to at least try."

"Well, let's get the crystal first," Eleonora said. She turned to Basil. "Feel like being the support?"

"Sure thing," Basil replied, crouching so that Myso could climb on his back. Felix followed suit, as did Eleonora. Isadora let out a big sigh, but climbed her way to the top, too. Dorabella scurried to the height of the stacked group, kneeling for just a brief moment on her mother's back before snatching up the crystal and allowing herself a controlled fall, landing flat-footed on the ground in just two hops. Isadora, Eleonora, Felix, and Myso tumbled to the ground soon after her.

"Give that to me, sweet child," Myso ordered, prompting Dorabella to quickly hand the crystal over to him. He looked it over, giving the green, brown, and gold-speckled crystal a few rubs with his thumb before turning it over to Felix.

"Let's go," Felix said.

"And how do we plan on doing that? Going back the way we came?" Isadora broke in.

"Ah, that's right," Myso said. "The other door."

"Assuming there is one," Eleonora chimed in. "But what about the gnomes?"

"I'm afraid that meeting up with my parents is going to have to take precedence over that," Felix said hurriedly. "But I promise you, darling. We'll get to the bottom of it at some point in the near future. Sooner or later."

Eleonora sighed. "All right," she replied. "How do we find this door, then?"

"I think I know," Basil interjected. "I'm not sure if you guys have noticed, but there's been a faint whispering the entire time we've been in here. I've been trying to decipher it, and it's almost like these skeletons are mumbling to each other. Maybe, just maybe, we could try to talk to them. Maybe they can tell us where this mystery exit is located."

"That's an excellent idea!" Myso exclaimed. "Don't you think so, Felix?"

"Indeed, if it works," Felix replied.

"But are any of us able to speak to the dead?" Eleonora broke in. "I've heard of beings having such capabilities, but by now surely wouldn't one of us have been aware of such a trait? It's like tree-whispering, is it not?"

"Yes, it is," Myso said. "I know that Narena has acted as a medium before, it's a shame she's not here with us."

"Probably for her benefit," Isadora grumbled, her stomach loudly growling. Eleonora was about to sigh, then suddenly became aware of her own hunger—painfully aware.

"Mommy, I'm hungry," Dorabella whined out of the blue.

Isadora wrapped her arm around her daughter. "I'm sorry, sweetie. I am, too."

"Eat some of the bread and berries, then!" Felix grumbled.

Basil furrowed his brow. "I think our sudden hunger has to do with where we are. These catacombs are not a positive place of light, that's for sure. These skeletal remains are slowly sucking away our energy."

"Which makes sense why the gnomes wouldn't want to stay here for very long," Eleonora said.

"But of course," Myso replied, "they had no choice. We need to get out of here. Immediately."

"One of us has to try to talk to these ghosts, or whatever they are," Felix demanded. "If no one volunteers, we will each try one by one—and keep trying until someone makes contact."

"Can I try?" Dorabella asked, her voice somewhat shaky and unsure.

"That actually might be a good idea," Myso said. "Children do maintain their spiritual abilities for a period of time before their souls become completely entwined in the realm of the living. And that includes seeing—and communicating with—souls that have passed over to the afterlife."

"Or refused to pass over," Dorabella said. "They're earthbound spirits. That one over there whispered that all these gnome skeletons are trapped here. They're trying to muster enough energy to get out, but they can't. Which is why they take energy from the living."

"Well, there you go!" Myso exclaimed, beaming. "Would you look at that!"

Isadora grinned from ear to ear. "That's *my* baby!" she cried, before saying, "Ask them for the exit!"

"They said that it should be obvious," Dorabella replied. "And that if the gnomes could figure it out, so could we."

"Is that some kind of dig at your own living kind?" Myso couldn't help but joke.

"Shh!" Felix scolded. "Dorabella, sweetheart. What else do they say?"

"The gnomes have fled the Forest completely, which is why the left the earth crystal here, for us to find and use. It's not likely they will return, and these spirits will not say where exactly they went, just that they're gone from the Forest. Supposedly that lantern we found back in the tunnel can provide more clues to their whereabouts."

"I'm afraid we don't have time to investigate that further. If we succeed in our current quest, perhaps we can look into that afterward. Anything else?"

"The door can be opened by something we already have," she replied.

"Something we already have?" Felix asked. "Do you think it means the crystal?"

"No," Dorabella said. "Otherwise the living gnomes wouldn't have left it here."

"What about that ash from that zombie nymph, Myso?" Basil broke in. "Didn't you say that it was part of a very powerful, ancient spell?"

"Good point, my dear friend!" Myso said. "I think I still have a little bit..." He rummaged around in his pockets. "Ah!" he declared, pulling out his tiny drawstring bag from his satchel. "I've got it!"

"They say you're right," Dorabella said. "You just have to draw a doorway with it."

Myso delicately stuck his index finger into the ash, gathered some on the tip, and began to draw a rectangular shape on the wall in front of him. Once he'd finished, he took a step back. The ash began to sizzle, forming an inverted hole in the wall. The light of the waning sun, the fluctuating greens of the trees and bushes, and the unmistakable smells of the Forest flooded the once-dingy chamber, prompting each and every member of the group to breathe sighs of relief.

"Goodbye skeletons!" Dorabella called on their way out. "Good luck escaping your tomb!"

"That was nice to say," Isadora said, beaming with pride. "I wish those ghosts the very best, as well."

"As do we all," Eleonora said with a smile directed at her sister. "It's a shame they are stuck where they are."

"Some souls have lessons to learn that we cannot possibly understand," Myso said softly. "At least in this lifetime."

"Let's head toward Lapis Mountain," Felix broke in. "From the looks of it, we should be getting there shortly after dark, if we make haste."

"Then let's go," Eleonora replied. "We've got no time to waste."

Everyone looked at the married couple for a moment, then all broke out simultaneously into laughter at the rhyme. Such frivolity was needed, so desperately needed, at that very moment. And all were quite grateful for it.

CHAPTER 17

Narena kissed her husband goodbye, hugging him tightly before gently pulling away.

"I love you, Narena," Kellen said, lightly brushing the tips of his fingers down Narena's cheeks. "Be safe. Be protected. Okay?"

"You got it," Narena replied, holding back tears. "And I love you too, Kellen."

Kellen handed Narena the air crystal, which she delicately placed within the buttoned satchel that she kept secured to her belt. Shelley hopped over to where Kellen lied, hoisting him onto Earl's back. Kellen clutched tightly to his scruff before the fox took off up the stairs, quickly glancing in each direction before disappearing from sight. Once they'd gone, Narena turned to Hawthorne and Shelley.

"Guess it's just us, then," she lamented.

"Until you both have to leave the Fire Realm," Hawthorne finished. "You do know I can't leave, right?"

Narena sighed. "Unfortunately, yes. But I was hoping I was wrong about that."

"Come on," Hawthorne said. "Let's get that crystal, then I'll show you to the Earth Realm portal."

Narena and Shelley followed the salamander carefully and quietly up the staircase. They peeked into the hallway, scanning every angle before making their way to the Salamander King's bedroom.

"Why does he keep it in his bedroom?" Narena hissed as they crept through the doorway.

"Paranoia, I'm assuming," Hawthorne whispered back. "Clearly we are not the first ones to try to take it."

"I'll stay here and stand guard," Shelley offered. "If anyone comes, I'm scooping you up, Narena, and breaking through that window over there."

"Sounds dramatic, but fair," Hawthorne replied.

"I'll be ready for that in case it happens," Narena chuckled. "But hopefully it doesn't."

"I don't think anyone's here, actually," Hawthorne said, rummaging in the area around in King Augustine's bed, which consisted of a soft, mossy log with warm, slightly-damp dirt underneath. "Strange as it is... aha!" He pulled a golden-specked, iridescent crimson stone from deep within the soil.

"Nice work, Hawthorne," Narena said, beaming.

"Now let's get you two to that Earth Realm portal," Hawthorne replied, handing the fire crystal to Narena, who instantly secured it alongside the air crystal within her buttoned pocket. The salamander headed over to a small table that was placed next to a moss-covered sitting chair, and messed around with one of the legs. Out of nowhere, a hole dropped out from the bottom of the table, forming a rounded tunnel that appeared to curve around and down from the palace. "Follow me," he said.

Narena climbed into the hole, turning just in time to watch Shelley scrunch her feathers as closely to her body as she possibly could, attempting to squeeze her head into the entrance of the tunnel. "This is no place for me," the crow sighed. "Perhaps I should try to exit through the window, and meet you at the bottom."

"That might be better, as I'm not sure you'll fit in here," Narena said. "It looks pretty tight."

"I think I can use my beak to unlatch this window here," Shelley explained. "I'll be fine, I'll see you guys in a little bit."

"Okay, good luck!" Narena said.

"Yes, do be safe," Hawthorne added, before disappearing into the hole. Narena gave Shelley one last wave before following her salamander friend into the pitch black of the tunnel, wholly trusting and yet completely unknowing of where exactly the darkened path would lead.

After several moments of traveling blindly through the tunnel, Narena finally began to see distant blinks of light.

"Almost there," Hawthorne muttered. "You're doing great, Narena. It's hard to walk in complete blindness. My salamander eyes are far keener than yours, I'm afraid."

"I'm just grateful to have you with me," Narena replied. "I don't know where I'd be without you."

"I won't be with you anymore very soon. Because we'll be at the portal shortly upon exiting this hole."

Narena huffed. "I'll miss you, of course. Again."

"We'll find a way to visit each other."

"I hope so."

The light became brighter, and before she knew it, Narena was outside, the igneous pebbles crunching under her feet.

"Quick—the portal's just over here," Hawthorne hissed. Narena dashed after the slithering amphibian, who was moving swiftly.

Shelley, who must have been circling closely enough to have caught a glimpse of the nymph and salamander, soared down to the ground next to Narena and hopped alongside her.

"There it is, just climb up," Hawthorne pointed out, stretching one of his moist fingers at the swirling mass of energy atop the gnome-shaped lava rock that seemed to stare back down at them. "Take care, my dearest Narena. And thank you, Shelley, for keeping her safe. It was the utmost pleasure, as always."

"Thank you, Hawthorne!" Narena said, embracing her amphibious friend for one last time before climbing onto Shelley's back. "I'll see you soon. Hopefully."

"I'll be awaiting that time, whenever it may be," Hawthorne replied. "Goodbye Narena! Goodbye Shelley!"

"Goodbye!" Narena and Shelley called in unison. Shelley turned, flapping her wings to gain enough momentum to soar triumphantly into the vortex, allowing herself and Narena to be sucked within it before disappearing from Hawthorne's gaze completely.

Felix, Eleonora, Myso, Basil, Isadora, and Dorabella were well on their way to the location where they were supposed to meet Narena, Kellen, Earl, and Shelley. Emerson had found them once they had re-entered the Forest, and was circling over the group as they continued their journey. As they grew closer to Lapis Mountain, a sinking feeling was felt by all—though this time nobody chose to speak about the harrowing sensation that was nearly impossible to ignore.

"We're almost there," Felix reassured, keeping his hand on the small of Eleonora's back as they walked.

"I can't wait to see your mother and father," Eleonora whispered.

"That'll be a first!" Felix joked back, but then suddenly halted in his tracks.

Standing before the group, blocking the small hole where they had planned to squeeze in to meet the rest of their comrades, stood Elecampane, glaring daggers at them. How everyone knew it was him was unclear, but perhaps Elec simply gave off the impression that he was one of the Controllers. But for whatever reason, it was painfully apparent who he was—and why he was there.

"If you hand over the crystals," Elecampane spoke forcefully, "I will spare your lives and allow you a head start. If not," he sneered, "I'd say your goodbyes to each other now."

"We don't know what you're talking about," Myso said. "We know not of what crystals you speak. We are merely trying to find our way home."

"Lies," Elecampane replied with an eerie grin. "Though I was never one to believe that trolls were the most honest and upstanding of beings."

"You're going to eat your words for that one," Myso growled, his body puffing up in agitation. "But we cannot relinquish what we do not have."

"The truth is written all over the faces of these nymphs. At least nymphs are too innocent to believe the falsehoods you speak."

"You do realize that the magic you possess and are using to control innocent beings has been outlawed in this Forest," Eleonora snapped. "If you kill us, your time in this realm will be short-lived."

"Ah, the story of my existence thus far," Elecampane sighed. "Do you think the idea of that bothers me? Sheesh, nymphs are not only innocent and oblivious—they're downright stupid."

"How dare you!" Felix cried.

"She's not even a nymph," Isadora muttered under her breath, not expecting Elecampane to take notice of her utterance, and yet he did.

"What was that, pretty one?" he said. "She is not a nymph? So let me guess then—a wingless faery?" He laughed heartily, deep from his belly. "How terrible it must be—to wield all the power that comes along with having wings—only to have them chopped off, removed... How did you manage to do that, little one?"

"Stop mocking her, or be prepared to answer to me!" Felix shouted.

"Aw, someone's in love," Elec said, taking notice of the rings upon their tiny fingers. "Married? Betrothed? Oh my, I wonder how the Faery King took to this one!" He cackled obnoxiously, then suddenly knelt down, looking long and hard at Felix before moving on to Eleonora. "Wait," he said, "I think I know you two. Yes! That's right! You're the king and queen of the nymphs! Ha ha, my brother and sisters will be *quite* pleased to learn I was able to eliminate the entire royal line of Nymph Kingdom in one fell swoop!"

"Quit talking and do it then!" Felix ordered, sailing an arrow directly at Elecampane's face. The Controller saw it coming, managing to jerk his head to the right just quickly enough to avoid the sharp obsidian tip from slicing through his eye. The arrow sailed past his temple, grazing the skin just barely enough to draw a thin line of dark, crimson blood.

"Oh, now you've done it," Elec said. "Now I'm annoyed!"

Elecampane looked as though he was mustering energy within

himself for a brief moment, like a volcano preparing to erupt. He drew back his hands, twisting his wrists around to form a concentrated ball of smoky, condensed energy. It was charcoal-gray and musty, resembling the viscosity of toxic sludge, though still maintaining an airiness to its texture. Elec pulled his arms back and instantly snapped them forward, releasing the ball to fly at an incredible speed toward the group of small beings.

"Get out of the way!" Myso screamed, tackling both Isadora and Dorabella and successfully shoving them into a nearby bush. Felix jumped out of the line of fire, and shot two more arrows at Elecampane, one landing in the meatiest part of his thigh, and the other sinking into his right shoulder. Eleonora rushed up to the Controller, slashing her blade across his left Achille's tendon before rushing back to her husband. Basil wasted no time in spraying a forceful, pungent burst of his scent directly at Elecampane, causing him to whirl around in circles as he attempted to cover both his mouth and nose simultaneously while Emerson circled overhead, dropping his own form of "bombs" until he had no more to release from his body. The crow knew he would not stand a chance of fitting his body into the hole, so opted to wait in an old oak tree that overlooked the entrance to which the group was now in the process of rapidly entering.

"Everyone! Quick!" Felix shouted. "Get into the hole! Now!"

Basil scooped up Isadora and Dorabella onto his back, galloping as fast as his stubby skunk legs could carry him. He gave Myso a swift bump on the behind with the top of his head, shoving the puffed-up troll through the entrance before squeezing through himself. Eleonora dove in next, while Felix managed to soar one last arrow at Elecampane before darting through the hole himself. Felix's last arrow was more than true—its accuracy sliced further into Elecampane's already bleeding facial wound, wedging the arrow to a protrusion that resembled an attack from a porcupine quill. Gushes of blood dropped heavily to the ground amid wails and curses from Elecampane, which was the last sound the Nymph King heard before descending into the depths of the mountain's crevice.

Chapter 18

"Is that you, Felix?"

The familiar voice echoed through the cave, willing the group to draw further into the darkness. Though they could barely see a fox tail's length in front of them, the reverberation of Felix's name continued to pull them within the mountain, until finally a loud scuffling sounded as though it were just ahead, and the smallest sliver of light emanated from a crack on a rock wall that extended from floor to ceiling.

"Mother, is that you?" Felix asked, feeling around in front of him. A soft, warm hand grabbed onto his and squeezed.

"Your eyes will adjust to the darkness, give it a few moments," Narena said. "Is everyone with you?"

"Except Emerson," Myso piped up. "He's waiting outside, keeping watch."

"He'll have run into Shelley then, I imagine," Narena replied. "Good. I'm glad to hear they'll be together."

"Where's Father?" Felix inquired. "I don't feel his presence here. Is he coming soon?"

Narena smiled, though her son was unable to notice. "Your intuition is spot on. Your father is not here. He injured himself in the Salamander Palace's dungeon. Earl took him home so he could heal."

"I thought Kellen was a healer," Eleonora broke in. "Couldn't he have healed himself?"

"Unfortunately, no," Narena replied. "I wish it were that simple. I was hoping he might have a chance at facing the Controllers with us, but the more I think about his situation, the more I doubt that he'll be able to. It'd require nothing short of a miracle, at this point."

"Well, the most we can do now is send Father our healing prayers and hope for the best," Felix said. "In the meantime, we really have no time to waste. The Forest is falling apart, its time of reckoning is near. We must stop it before the damage is irrevocable."

"I don't know about you guys, but I can fully see now," Myso said.

"As can I," Felix chimed in. "Mother, have you checked out these caverns? Is there a way to go to where we need to go, or must we go back to the hole we came in from? Hopefully, our Controller friend is not still waiting for us."

"Luckily, I don't think we'll need to," Narena replied. "I came in from another side, and I did happen to pass by a stone hallway where I heard many distinct voices coming through the rocks. I think it was where the Controllers are hiding out, and they definitely have the Elder Triage. I'm pretty sure I heard additional voices too, though I'm not sure whose they were."

"So, we should be able to reach the Controllers' lair by going back the way you came, Narena?" Myso reiterated.

"Right," Narena replied. "Sorry, I'm a bit frazzled. It's tough being by yourself in trying times like these. I wish Kellen were here."

"You've always been strong on your own, too, Mom," Felix said. "Don't ever forget that." Narena wrapped her arms around her son, beaming. Felix's face flushed, before saying, "All right, then. Let's go save some witches, shall we?" He allowed an enormous grin to overtake his face, which was fairly uncommon for him under normal circumstances. "Oh yeah," he chuckled. "And let's save our Forest, too."

"Aye, aye!" Myso declared. "I am ready, King Felix."

"As am I," Basil piped up.

"And me, too!" Eleonora exclaimed.

"I suppose I'm as ready as I'll ever be," Narena said.

Myso turned to Isadora and Dorabella with the most solemn expression either female faery had ever witnessed upon his face. "I'd prefer if you two stayed close to me and Basil," the troll said.

"We have our weapons," Isadora replied.

"It's not always weapons that you have to worry about," Myso retorted.

"I'll try to stay out of the way, but I want to help if I can," Dorabella said.

"I'd just feel better if you two stuck close to me and Basil," the troll repeated.

"Just stay behind me," Basil chimed in. "And if you see an opening to attack—take it! I'll be right there, so don't worry."

"Everyone is going to be fine," Eleonora said, as if trying to convince herself. "Just fine."

"We all just need to remember to stay open to messages from our higher selves," Narena explained. "You never know when your intuition can provide insight that can help you out. Don't ignore what you're feeling! That's the most valuable advice I can give."

"And we appreciate that a lot," Isadora replied. "I know at least I do. Truly." She provided the older female nymph with a gentle, genuine smile, one that caused Narena to look a bit surprised. Her eyes widened, then her brow instantly softened.

"Thank you, Isadora," she said softly, patting the faery's shoulder.

"Okay!" Felix declared. "Is everybody ready? Let's move!"

Narena and Felix took the lead, with Narena silently pointing out the direction for Felix to walk.

"There will be more light in just a moment, here," Narena whispered. "Right after we turn this corner..."

Narena turned the corner just a split second before Felix, but her sudden gasp prompted the group to hang back, though Felix managed to peer around the corner to witness the same sight as his mother. A slew of zombies—mostly nymphs, gnomes, and trolls—were furiously marching through the cavern, headed straight for the pathway that the group had been traveling, and blocking the way to the Controllers' lair that was only a mere ten or twenty fox tail's lengths away from where the group was.

Felix held out his fingers, mouthing a countdown until everyone would come charging around the corner, pick a zombie to slay, but most of all—attempt to safely reach the exit. Narena fervently muttered prayers to the Higher Spirits under her breath, intensifying the effect of her son's order.

"Three..." Felix said. "Two... *One!*"

The group followed the Nymph King, stampeding around the corner wielding blades, arrows, and in Basil's case, teeth and claws. The zombies—two trolls, a gnome, and two nymphs—instantly took notice of the beings, increasing their shuffles in speed and fervor.

"I know these trolls," Myso groaned. "I've known them since I was a kid! I went to school with them."

"They are no longer trolls!" Basil called at his friend. "Do not think of them as such!"

Felix's heart sank when he realized that he recognized the two nymphs that were furiously headed his way. He'd played Acornball with them many times as a child, and now they were a well-known set of warrior brothers who were guards of one of the Nymph Kingdom's lookout towers. They would have been comrades to Leroy, the zombie nymph that Myso and Basil had faced, though that time seemed ever so distant from their current predicament.

One of the zombie brothers lunged at Felix, prompting him to instantly release an arrow, which soared through the thick cavern atmosphere and cleanly sliced into the zombie's left eye socket. The arrow must have not punctured the brain or severed the spine, for the zombie only stopped his advance for a brief moment before continuing.

Realizing he had little distance to procure another arrow, Felix whipped out his blade from its sheath, managing to swing it just as the arrow-eyed zombie attempted to tear at his face. The blade cut into the zombie nymph's throat, discharging a black and crimson coagulum of thickened blood and putrid-smelling grime that densely cascaded to the cavern floor. The zombie fell as his undead brother looked on in horror, his eyes glazed and distant. The brother snarled, accelerating rigorously at the Nymph King and slapping the blade from his hands. Felix wasted no time in throwing a swift punch that knocked the zombie backwards, though the undead nymph did not, in any way, halt his advance. The zombie nymph tackled Felix, shoving his body to the ground and attempting to lift his shoulders up so he could slam the king's body down again repeatedly.

"Felix!" Eleonora shouted, rushing to her husband's side. She tried to pull the zombie nymph off of him, but found, even for an undead being, he was far stronger than she was. "Myso!" the Nymph Queen cried desperately, though upon turning her head to see where the troll was, she found that he was fully engaged in battle against the two zombie trolls. She would have to handle the zombie nymph herself.

Eleonora raised her blade high above her head, holding it there briefly before slamming her clenched fist downwards, stabbing directly into the zombie nymph's cervical vertebra, severing it perfectly between two of the bones. The zombie twitched, then thrashed wildly for a moment before slumping his weight heavily upon Felix. Using all his strength, and with the help of his wife, the Nymph King was able to push the zombie's body off of him, and the married couple rushed to help their friends.

Myso was comparable in size to the two undead trolls, even when all trolls in question were puffed up in agitation. Both zombie trolls seemed more interested in fighting Myso than Basil, though each attack made by the foes were quickly intercepted by the skunk, who used his size, stench, canine teeth, and sharp claws to bat them away from his friend. At one point, one of the zombie trolls tried to sneak in a bite to the back of Myso's neck, but out of nowhere flew Dorabella, piercing her blade directly into the zombie troll's lower spine. The zombie flinched, and whirled around howling while Dorabella attempted to retrieve her blade from his flesh. But the zombie was quicker than the little faery, whacking her out of the way as if she were nothing more than an annoying, buzzing insect. Dorabella went flying freely for a moment before flapping her wings and righting herself, but it appeared the zombie was done with her. The undead troll grinned as he turned back to Myso and dove forward once again.

Myso wielded his blade, creeping closer towards the zombie. "There might be a chance for you," he said to the creature. "I urge you—retreat now! Your soul can still be saved!"

The zombie troll said nothing, only sneered an eerie grin, dripping with drool. With a monstrous growl, he stormed at Myso, teeth protruding from his mouth and elongated fingernails slashing through the otherwise still air. Myso jumped back, just narrowly avoiding a bite that surely would have lopped off his left ear. Nevertheless, he keeled to the ground as a result of the attack, the unforgiving zombie looming over him. Myso furiously swiped his blade through the air in front of him, warning the zombie to keep back, but of course, the undead troll was not inclined to oblige.

The zombie troll prepared himself to pounce, his eyes glazed, yet focused on his prize. He grabbed Myso by the collar of his tunic, pulling him towards his stinking breath with unforeseen strength. He lifted his hand, fingernails pointed towards the living troll's eye sockets, and was just about to descend a deadly blow when out of nowhere, Isadora came soaring across the battlefield, her shiny, barely used blade reflecting the small amount of light visible within the cavern. She plunged the point of her blade as powerfully and deeply as she could into the zombie's neck, twisting it as she landed on the ground. The sheer force of the strike was enough to finish the creature, the final turn of the sharpened metal nearly decapitating the zombie completely. Myso sat up, eyes wide and mouth agape in utter shock yet pleasant surprise at the faery's attack.

"Wow," was all the troll could muster. "Nicely done."

"Mommy, you saved Myso!" Dorabella cried, rushing to her mother's side. Upon noticing her blade still sticking from the zombie troll's back, she pulled it off and wiped it on the deceased troll's tunic before sliding it back into her belt loop.

Isadora turned bright red, and rolled her eyes as if her rescue had been nothing more than a simple task. "It's no big deal," she replied. "Basil was helping Narena, anyway."

Myso pulled himself up to his feet. "Well," he remarked with a sly grin spreading across his face. "Let's help him, then, shall we, Miss Warrior Faery?"

Isadora beamed, now feeling her ears getting hot. "Sounds good," she squeaked out. "Dorabella, stay close to me."

"After *that* display of heroism, I'd surely oblige, too!" Myso called back, already on the other side of the cavern, blade in hand.

Indeed, Basil had intervened on the battle being waged between Narena and the last remaining zombie—an adolescent gnome who, despite being a female, was graced with the slightest beard, though in the dim lighting of the cave it only appeared to be a somewhat overgrown five o'clock shadow. The zombie gnome had been proving to be not only a well-trained warrior in life, but wholly relentless, and it looked as though the fight was clearly taking its toll on the mature female nymph.

With one swift swipe of the paw, Basil knocked the zombie gnome to the ground, but she quickly pulled herself up and came right back at Narena, almost as if she hadn't even noticed that the skunk was there. Narena successfully blocked an open-mouthed attack, but each time she narrowly avoided the gnome's advance, the zombie only seemed to come back stronger. But the odds were stacked against the poor undead gnome, indeed, because it wasn't too long after Myso's arrival that the undead gnome lied motionless on the cavern floor, the troll's blade cleaved through her neck from behind. Then the cave became unnervingly still and silent.

"Do you think there's more?" Eleonora hissed.

"I don't know..." Felix trailed off, suddenly alerted by a noise coming from the exit to the cave.

A blackened silhouette blocked the light that had been pouring in, standing about as tall as a male warrior nymph but adorned with outstretched, wispy wings. Behind the figure, countless pulsating shadows were visible in the background, their ravenous snarls audible and echoing through the darkness. Felix held up his hand to his brow, frantically trying to get a better view of the menacing presence that now threatened his group.

"Well, well, well," the shadow spoke. "I didn't expect to find *this* many survivors, and would you believe it! I even recognize some of you."

"Oh no..." Isadora gulped, though nobody paid any mind to her words.

Felix squinted his eyes. "Wait, I know you," he said. "Your voice sounds familiar. Lucian? Is that you?"

Lucian, King of the Faeries, let out a long and exaggerated sigh. "My reputation precedes me, as usual," he muttered. He stepped further in the cave, ordering whatever minions were behind him to keep back for the time being. His eyes scanned the group, stopping only when they reached Isadora. "Isadora," was all he said, prompting the rest of the group to exchange confused glances. Isadora averted her eyes from the king's glare, and said nothing. Lucian's gaze slid over to Dorabella, where he cocked his head slightly, opening his mouth as if he meant to say something more before offering the faery child a wink.

"Don't speak to her," Isadora said forcefully. "Don't even look at her!"

"You seem to have forgotten," Lucian sneered, "that I am a king.

And not just any king... *your* king. You'd do well to hold your tongue in my presence. If you know what's good for you, that is."

"The few times I've been in your presence," Isadora retorted, "it has *never* been good for me."

"Aw, that's too bad. Because I had a good time. But then I grew bored of you and your incessant chatter, which I'm sure comes as no surprise to your friends here."

"You make me sick."

"That's what I heard happened in your first trimester."

"How would you even know? You excommunicated me!"

"Wait, what's going on here?" Eleonora interjected. "Isadora, I thought you said you didn't know King Lucian."

"I never said that," Isadora replied. "Dorabella did. I didn't say anything."

"Probably the first time in your entire life that you didn't speak," Lucian snorted.

"No one asked you!" Isadora cried. "Just go away and leave us be!"

Lucian sauntered closer to the group, a creepy smile plastered on his face. "I'm afraid I can't do that. My transformation is nearly complete. Soon I will have gained enough power to enforce the laws of the Forest that were deemed unsuitable for harmonious existence generations ago. Once I kill all of you, I will go back to helping the Controllers finish their task of bringing the Forest back to its original, *delightfully* negative chaos that it once was... before the ogres were removed, before the Controllers were cast away... before any of this nonsensical balance was enacted and continually enforced for all these dreadfully long and tedious generations. But now that I know my interest here is at risk, well, I must step in, just this once." He laughed. "Of course, I did have to step in previously as well, when my father was failing to accept the progression of the faeries. How simple it was to remove him from the equation and claim the throne for myself, as I was entitled. Just a pinch of oleander in his morning tea was enough to do the trick, and before I could say 'hail Gorgon'—I was wearing the crown.

"I'm sure by now you've realized that it was I, King Lucian, who set the Controllers free from their bonds. Horrible to keep such influential beings locked away like that. We should be celebrating them, not sealing away their magic. But I digress..."

Lucian paced around as he spoke, his thumb and forefinger carefully rubbing his chin.

"To apprentice under Gorgon, there are a strict set of rules one must adhere to, at all times, before even the slightest consideration can be given. You do not speak of your apprenticeship, and go to great lengths to keep it hidden. Most kings assume I apprenticed under Arepo, but luckily for me—and Gorgon—Higher Spirits are forbidden to speak.

"I gained enough knowledge and power to enact the spell that Gorgon helped me complete, the spell that would bring the Controllers back to the Forest. In return, I was promised the position of Supreme King, my word absolute over all of the kingdoms, to be enforced by Gorgon himself, and his strongest minions, of course.

"The ogres must return, it has been decreed by Gorgon, who is arguably the most powerful of the Spirits, especially since this time of reckoning began. And with great power, comes great responsibility, and therefore to exclude the ogres from the resources of this Forest when they are completely equal to the beings of light is beyond ludicrous. In fact, it's outright preposterous."

"Nice vocabulary," Isadora snorted. "Did you look those up today, before you came here?"

"Are you completely blind to the fact that the ogres destroyed and polluted the resources of the Forest to the near brink of extinction?" Narena broke in. "How is a species entitled to resources when they've proven time and time again to abuse them? Complete disregard of the state of the Forest is not a Yew-given right!"

Lucian glared at Narena. "You—nymph—have no idea what you're talking about. The ogres were the likeness of Gorgon, the species he reveled in creating. You do realize that Celandine is Gorgon's most prized daughter, right? He basically adopted the siblings when they engaged in the ritual to declare complete and utter loyalty to him, apprenticing under him for generations, not to mention absorbing as much power as he was willing to give them.

"But then Celandine's supposed best friend Nessaba cast Gorgon's ogres away, murdering hundreds, if not thousands, in the process. After swearing her loyalty to Gorgon, she turns around and betrays him, apparently deciding to go over to the light. She tried to make Celandine join her, but ultimately our lady made the correct choice. You can imagine the strain it put on Celandine and Gorgon's relationship! Perhaps that's why Celandine is so invested in bringing them back."

"I knew you were a piece of scat," Isadora said. "I knew it the moment you asked me if I wanted to see your collection of figurines made in your likeness."

"Ew..." Eleonora remarked, exchanging a disgusted look with Narena, who was trying not to laugh. She'd always had a habit of laughing during awkward situations, but she also never missed a chance to enjoy any brief, fleeting moments of humor in times of peril.

Lucian stopped, and abruptly turned, staring deeply into Dorabella's eyes and causing hers to lock with his as if in some kind of trance.

Isadora grabbed her daughter, pulling her as far away from Lucian as she possibly could. "Leave her alone!" she yelled, slapping her hand over Dorabella's eyes and curling herself and her daughter into a fetal position, as they were quickly surrounded by Myso and Basil.

Lucian cackled wickedly. "I can very easily take her, you know," he mocked. "I have as much a right to her as you do."

"Get away from her!" Eleonora cried. "You have no ownership of them just because they are faeries!"

Lucian cocked his head and stared at Eleonora for only a brief moment before lowering his voice to a rasping growl and uttering the words that would cause everyone in the group to collectively gasp in complete and utter shock.

"Oh, but I do claim ownership of these faeries—at least the child. Did you oblivious nymphs not know? Dorabella is *my* daughter. *My* flesh and blood. She is *mine*, and I have every intention of taking her with me."

CHAPTER 19

"You can't have her!" Isadora screamed. "You haven't even been in her life! Didn't you say that you never wanted it to be known that she was your child? That's what you told me when you kicked me out of Faery Kingdom, or have you forgotten? She is *my* baby, I raised her... She doesn't even know you!"

"Of course Dorabella would want to know who her father is," Lucian sneered. "And of course I wouldn't want everyone to know that I had fathered a child out of wedlock. We were young and stupid back then, Isadora, and it's insulting that you act as though I disregarded you and cast you out completely, when we both know that's false. But now... now I am King of the Faeries, and I want my bloodline returned to me! Dorabella would have a great life with me at the palace, it'd be a shame for you—her mother—to cause her to miss out."

"Where would Isadora go?" Eleonora broke in. "To the palace, as well?"

"No way," Lucian snickered. "It'd be easier if she were simply out of the picture. I'll tell everyone she died during this whole ordeal, and I, kindhearted as I am, decided to adopt the little orphan. It's tragic, really; a daughter to see her mother perish right before her very eyes. Traumatizing for a little girl, indeed. It's a good thing I'll be there to comfort her and raise her properly."

Eleonora felt her face grow so hot that it felt as though it were on fire. She grasped her sister's hand and furiously stepped forward before saying, "Isadora is an exceptional parent—better than you'll ever be. She is the only parent Dorabella has ever needed, and will ever need. You are toxic to an adult being, let alone to an innocent, impressionable child. You will *never* take Dorabella! The only way would be over my dead body, so I guess if you're going to kill my sister, you'd better kill me with her."

"And me," Myso broke in.

"And me!" said Basil.

"Me, too," chimed in Felix.

"And me!" Narena cried.

Lucian gave an unsettling smirk before replying, "Well, I guess that settles it then. I'll have to kill all of you. Except for my own flesh and blood, of course." He turned slightly around to address the army of faery zombies that were pacing behind him. "Capture the child and bring her to me. As for the rest—kill them."

The zombies suddenly became alert, as if drawn out of some kind of unwilling torpor. They started to shuffle at an alarming speed towards the group, who readied their weapons for battle against the undead once again.

There were probably at least a dozen of zombie faeries, most of them male, though a fair few were female. They were likely warriors, and Eleonora cringed as she began to recognize some familiar faces from her own childhood, growing up in Faery Kingdom.

"Form a circle around Dorabella," Felix ordered. "Don't let any of them in!"

The zombies reached the group, and each member began to fight back. Felix quickly severed the spine of the first zombie to approach him, and eagerly moved on to the second. Eleonora was able to knock down one of the female zombies, slashing the undead's legs and successfully thwarting her advance. She was not inclined to straight-out kill her attackers, especially if they were female, but knew deep down that she probably would not be given the luxury of merely wounding every foe that came her way. At some point, despite her strong desire to not kill a member of her former kind, she would likely have to.

Myso and Basil were offing zombie faeries left and right, so quickly in fact that it started to make Lucian visibly uncomfortable. As each zombie fell, Lucian grew more and more irritated. Finally, upon realizing that he would lose most—if not all—of his minions, he called out another command, but not before rolling his eyes to the back of his head and appearing to summon—or possibly even channel—a Spirit that, although was currently in possession of another soul, maintained an omnipotent presence far more powerful that even he, the Faery King could ever possibly imagine.

"Valerian, hear you me!"

Lucian seemed to snap back to reality. He watched as the group battled his zombie minions for a moment, eerily smiling and muttering to himself as if there were someone else there with him—or perhaps, within him. In the midst of battling the zombie faeries, the tight circle around Dorabella had disbanded, and it didn't take long for an opening to appear just large enough for the Faery King to dash through at an almost impossible speed, fluttering his wings to gain faster momentum. Lucian burst through the circle, snatched up Dorabella, and soared back to the safe zone behind his slew of zombies. He laughed loudly enough for the members of the group to take notice, dangling Dorabella in mid-air by the wing.

"He's got Dorabella!" Isadora screeched, trying to rush across the cavern, blade slashing in Lucian's direction. "Give her back, you disgusting excuse for a faery!"

Lucian snickered. "Come and get her, sweetheart," he mocked. "If you can get past my army, that is. Have you even mentioned to your little friends that you were aware of the court's plans to increase the faeries' influence?"

"I knew nothing!" Isadora shrieked. "You hid me and Dorabella away in shame, how could I know the extent of what you and the courts were trying to do?"

"You knew enough. All faeries were aware of the need for such diplomacy."

"I am merely a citizen! A bystander with no power of her own, no control over the actions of the courts!" She turned to the members of her group, who had formed a blockage in front of her as she spoke to Lucian over the heads of the undead army, still trying to slow the zombies' advances. "Eleonora, you must know that I never would have wanted this! You know that the majority of the faeries are good! If they have supported Lucian, it was under some form of deception by him or by the courts! Faeries truly only want what is right, they only wanted the purest balance for the Forest!"

"I know that, my sister," Eleonora said. And she meant it.

"I will never call you my daddy!" Dorabella suddenly shouted angrily at Lucian. "You're nothing but a bad being! And if you were smart enough to know *anything* about the Forest's history, you would know that the faeries were the ones who aided Nessaba in the spell that eliminated the ogres!"

"You're but a child! What do you know, anyway?" Lucian retorted. "*Everyone* knows it was the gnomes that helped Nessaba. And look at what happened to them. Last I heard, they were going the way of the salamanders! Does *anybody* know where King Gregor is?" He snickered.

"There were gnomes, but there were also many powerful, influential faeries!" Dorabella shot back. "If you had ever read a book in your life, you'd know that! Nessaba and numerous beings of light—including *faeries*—performed the spell that enacted the Yew to fly over the entire Forest, destroying the weak ogres and hypnotizing the few that were strong, prompting them to march to their entrapment in that faraway mountain. This is from a history book that I procured from *your* library!"

In the background, Narena chuckled, trying to hold back her smile as her mind raced, desperately searching for a solution to their current predicament as she beamed with pride at Dorabella's intelligence and forcefulness. In many ways, she reminded Narena of herself.

"Books are nothing but tales of lies. You, my child, need to grow up."

"I will *never* be your child!"

"What if we surrender?" Narena asked out of the blue, all the while slashing her blade to keep a zombie at bay. "You'll be able to save the rest of your army, since we will surely defeat the rest of them, and then you can let the Controllers deal with us. We'd be out of your hair, and you will likely receive praise from your superiors."

"I doubt the Controllers want us dead straight away," Myso chimed in as he continued fighting a relentless zombie. "I'm sure they'd rather finish us off themselves, especially since we've caused them so much trouble lately."

Lucian thought about that for a moment, and appeared to have a two-way conversation, in hissing and muttering to himself. Finally, he responded.

"All right zombies!" he shouted. "Secure these beings. We will bring them to the Controllers." He turned to the group. "And if there's any— and I mean *any*—resistance, you have my permission to kill the being in question."

The zombies let out a guttural murmur, which Lucian clearly took as acquiescence. "You," he ordered a particularly large zombie, "take their weapons. All of them. The rest of you, grab a being and follow me."

The group willingly handed over their weapons, though nobody even reached for the smaller blades that Felix had always prompted the members of his army to carry, securely hidden within their boots. At least the members of the group would have them in case they were needed, and from the looks of the situation, they most likely would be. The group allowed the zombies to herd them behind Lucian as he sashayed his way through the tunnels of the mountain's cave, all the while with Dorabella still tucked sideways under his arm.

After a few moments of spelunking deeper into the cave, Lucian turned and gave the zombies behind him a nod. An opening to a larger, more lit cavern became visible, though a trio of reebobs sat crouched in front, blocking the group from entering.

"Ah, it's only you," one of the reebobs growled upon seeing Lucian's face. The reebob scanned the group before commenting, "Looks like you outdid yourself. Go on in."

The reebobs moved out of the way, and Lucian strolled into the cavern, head held high.

"Well, look at what we have here!"

The voice was all too familiar to Eleonora, and though she didn't quite have a good view of who was speaking, it sent a chill up her spine that resulted in her entire body breaking out in goosebumps. She knew that she'd heard that voice somewhere before, and as the speaker in question came more into view, Eleonora couldn't help but gasp at the sight of who it was.

It was none other than the strange, eerie woman who had helped Eleonora when she had been in the Forest alone, and while that was not so long ago, it felt as though it had been an eternity. Next to her stood the Controller who had attacked the group outside the mountain just before they had reconvened with Narena, as well as two other humans who were presumably the other Controllers. All four of the siblings maintained a presence about them, a fortitude that was not only frightening, but an overall force to be reckoned with. Eleonora didn't know if she should regret offering to surrender to Lucian in order to face the Controllers, but all she knew was that defeating this ancient, powerful warlock family would be no easy task.

The woman, who was dressed in a red cloak, knelt down for a better look at the group of beings. Her eyes scanned across each individual, stopping only at Eleonora, who was desperately trying to avoid eye contact.

"Hey," the woman said, more softly that any of the beings would have expected. "I know you. Esmeralda, right?"

"I'm afraid not," Eleonora squeaked back.

The woman stood upright, now looming over the group, her shadow casting a darkness and an overall sense of imminent dread upon them. "You don't remember me?" she snapped, her tone suddenly more cold and unfeeling. "Because I certainly remember you."

"Perhaps I've just forgotten," Eleonora said quietly.

"Forgotten the one who spared your life?" snorted Celandine. "How ungrateful."

"And that's my sister's biggest annoyance," Elecampane broke in contemptuously, a bloodied bandage wrapped around his head. "Ungratefulness."

"Funny then, isn't it?" Myso broke in out of the blue. "That you—a Controller of all beings—would stress gratefulness when it was *you* who never ceased to greedily attempt to take any power anywhere you possibly could. Had you been grateful at all for the fair amount of power you were given as a witch—and *then* as a warlock—you would have not been cast out with the ogres!"

"I find it odd that a *troll* would ever assume that I'd revel in his uneducated judgments of why I do what I do. You do know what they say about opinions, right?" She turned to Mullein and Elecampane. "What do you think? Shall we toss them to the possessed Elder Triage and let them go to town on them? Or should we keep them separate until we have further use for their existences?"

"Well, they have caused us quite a bit of grief," Mullein said.

"Not to mention all the time we've been delayed in our spell because of them," Bellis pointed out.

"And look at what they did to me!" complained Elecampane, holding up his index finger to draw attention to his bandaged face.

"Well, I suppose that settles it, then," Celandine sighed. "Let's see how well they fare against the Elder Triage."

"Wait," Mullein broke in. "What about the realm crystals?"

Celandine half-smirked, portraying a sense of beauty and charisma mixed with an unyielding power that only prompted a deepening sense of dread to the members of the group.

"That's right," she agreed, focusing her glare upon the group. "Hand 'em over."

"How do you know we even have them?" Felix said. "Wouldn't it be safe to assume that we were unable to procure the crystals from the realms? None of the kings were willing to give them up, even for the sake of the Forest."

"It might be safe to assume that," Celandine replied. "But I know all too well that it isn't true. I *know* you have them, and if they are not placed in my hand by the time I count to ten... Well, I'm not sure you're going to like what will happen after that."

Felix exchanged glances with his wife, his mother, Myso, and finally Basil. "We don't have them," Myso assured. "If we did, wouldn't we have used them already?"

"Not likely, given your predicament," Mullein said. "You best listen to my sister, if you know what's good for you. Hand 'em over, and we'll give you more of a fighting chance against the possessed Elder Triage."

"It won't be difficult to search you," Elecampane broke in. "And it would be *so* tragic for you to be squished into a pulp from us even trying."

"And you wouldn't want anything to happen to this precious little one," Bellis added, nodding at Lucian, who sat aside Dorabella, his hand clutched tightly onto her wrist, with all the beings' weapons piled high to his side.

"We need to just trust that we'll be able to get the crystals back at the right time, when we need them," Eleonora whispered into her husband's ear. "We have to do it, they've got Dorabella!"

"They've got us, too!" Felix hissed back.

Celandine swept her arm through the air, sending a wave of fire that encircled the group of beings, locking them within the flames. She bent down, her face illuminated as orange and red flickering shadows danced hypnotically in her eyes. Her hand lowered into the circle, open-palmed and emanating its own heat.

"Ahem," Celandine said. "The crystals? Or do I need to start counting?"

Felix furrowed his brow in frustration, then exhaled loudly before rummaging in his pocket. Narena took the cue from her son and reached into her own pocket, with mother and son simultaneously revealing the four glimmering crystals in the palms of their hands. Celandine's eye widened at the sight, though she wasted no time in snatching the crystals and grasping them tightly within one of her fists.

"We can use these to further strengthen our spell," she said with a smirk. "So, thank you."

She placed the crystals on a stalagmite that was flattened at the top, forming a make-shift shelf. Then, she muttered a few inaudible words under her breath, and shot her hand forward, sending a raging ball of fire soaring onto the shelf, where it landed flatly on the surface, flickering sparks in every direction. Celandine picked up the realm crystals once again, dropping each one within the depths of the fireball before turning back to her siblings.

"All right," she sighed, suddenly sounding bored with the situation. "Throw them in with the Elder Triage. I'm ready for them to die."

CHAPTER 20

"Wait! Don't do this!" Felix shouted to no avail as each member of the group was plucked, one by one, from the circle of fire and clasped within a Controller's hand so only their heads were visible. Basil made a formidable attempt at fighting back, using his teeth, claws, and even musk, but Bellis was quick to enact a water barrier around his body that rendered his attacks useless.

The Controllers laughed among themselves as they made their way to the back of the cavern, turning a corner before entering another cave that was not as well lit as the previous one. Menacing scuffles and incomprehensible murmuring could be heard, though once the Controllers had fully entered the room, little beings within their hands, the noises stopped.

"It's feeding time!" Elecampane announced, waving his hand across what appeared to be some kind of energetic barrier, before dropping the beings over the enormous stalagmites that Mullein had forged from the bedrock below the cavern floor, which now formed the bottom of a cage that held the Elder Triage. The other Controllers took turns dropping the rest of the group into the enclosure, finally tossing Basil within his ball of water over the top. The ball burst upon contact with the ground, releasing the skunk and splashing his companions.

The group huddled closely together, Isadora quietly weeping over the separation from her daughter. Eleonora, on the other hand, had a fiery determination to rescue her niece from Lucian.

"We need to meditate," she said. "We need help from the Higher Spirits."

"She's right," Narena agreed. "I think they're our only hope at this point."

"What about the Elders?" Felix asked.

Before anyone was able to answer, a towering figure stepped out of the darkness and slowly came more clearly into view. A long, white beard cascaded from his chin, and what appeared to be a normally friendly face was plastered with an almost evil, unfeeling scowl. The most striking feature of this looming figure was his eyes—once a sparkling green, they now glowed a putrid yellow, unfocused and intent on imminent chaos.

"It's Magus..." Eleonora whispered, almost unable to believe what she was seeing.

"It's not really Magus," Myso replied quickly. "We have to get out of this pen. This possessed coven will kill us without thinking twice about it. They no longer know who we are, let alone that we were once allies."

"Or friends," Felix finished.

"Is there no hope to release them from the entities that possess them?" Narena said. "There must be! Let me think for a moment..."

"We don't have a moment, Mother!" Felix cried. "Look, there's two more!"

Surely enough, two more crouching figures emerged, looking

somewhat like humans that once were the witches Lorella and Rhoslina, though now aged almost beyond recognition, and, of course, adorned with similar sets of sinister yellow eyes.

"They're not just possessed by entities," Myso gulped upon studying the once-human witches and wizard closely. "No, no. Not just any entities, indeed."

"What do you mean?" Eleonora asked, amid a lump forming in the back of her throat as she gazed up at the tremendous sight before her. "What else would they be possessed by?"

"Under Spirits," Narena broke in, her voice shaky.

"Which ones?" Felix hissed. "Agrimon was destroyed with Labete during the falling. That would leave only Doppel and Valerian, since Gorgon would be too powerful of a Spirit to even bother with possessing a bunch of magical humans, right?"

"I don't know..."

"All right, I think we can go start our spell," Celandine interjected loudly to her siblings through the hushed whispers among the members of the group. "Looks like Doppel and Valerian have this one under control."

Bellis raised an eyebrow. "Are you sure, my sister? Wouldn't it be wiser to watch their demise, just to ensure that..."

"Are you questioning my methods?" snapped Celandine. "These are the Under Spirits we're talking about, not some run of the mill negative entity like The Second."

"But remember what happened to The Second?" Mullein piped up.

Celandine sighed loudly and exaggeratedly. "One of you stay here and watch, then. Because I've waited long enough to enact this spell, and I don't know about you, but I'm ready to inherit the immense power that I've been waiting for generations to receive. As have all of you."

"We are all required to be present for the spell," Elecampane said. "And I know I would be the one to stay, and I'd rather not."

"Okay, okay," Celandine groaned. "Lucian!"

Lucian popped his head into the cavern room. "Yes?"

"I need you to make sure that the Under Spirits successfully kill each and every being in there," Celandine ordered. "When it's done, come back, because we could use your help for the end of the spell."

"You got it, my lady," Lucian replied with a grin, dragging Dorabella and the pile of weapons into the room. He looked to Bellis, pointing at his daughter. Bellis replied with a slight nod and flicked her fingers into the corner, sending a ball of water soaring at Dorabella and trapping her body within it from the neck down.

"That way she'll be able to breathe," Bellis said with a laugh, before following her sister and two brothers back to the larger cavern.

While all this had been going on, Myso and Narena had wasted no time hiding behind Felix and Basil and allowing themselves to fall into their deep meditative states. The Elder Triage still loomed over them, presumably deciding how to kill them, or perhaps taking in the sight of the little Forest beings from their newfound, possessed-bodied perspectives. But for whatever reason, it provided Myso and Narena just enough time to send out pleas for help from Sator and Arepo, and luckily for them, the Higher Spirits were so invested in the matter that they responded almost immediately.

In the furthest corner of the cavern, just barely out of vision though still detectable, two presences began to slowly morph from a faint mist into more articulate forms. One, the distinct shape of a mature buck, kicked his hoof furiously as he came completely into view. The other, shorter and rounder in overall build, altered himself from amorphous to the form of a turtle. It was, without a doubt, the Higher Spirits Sator and Arepo, and their presences conveyed nothing more than pure, unadulterated love, entities of guidance and direction.

"Look!" Narena cried upon opening her eyes and noticing the silhouettes. "We are in the presence of Higher Spirits!"

"How did they come so quickly?" Isadora inquired.

"They must have been paying attention," Myso replied.

"With good reason," Basil finished.

Magus, Lorella, and Rhoslina, in their possessed states, saw the embodiments of the Higher Spirits as well, because they collectively began hissing and growling as if the mere presence of the Higher Spirits mortally offended them. The Elder Triage crouched simultaneously, and began creeping to the edge of the make-shift cage in which they were being kept. The members of the group scurried to get out of their way, shifting themselves to the darkest corner of the enclosure.

"What are Sator and Arepo going to do?" Felix asked his mother.

"I'm not sure..." Narena trailed off, her eyes fixated on the Spirits.

Lucian, who had been sitting with Dorabella near the entrance to the room, suddenly leaped up from his seat, haphazardly dragging his daughter to stand directly in front of Sator and managing to burst the water bubble that the child was entrapped within. But upon looking directly into the Higher Spirit's eyes, Lucian's body instantly stiffened, as if the mere sight of the Spirit prompted his mind to shut down. Dorabella shook herself loose, scooting backwards as far away from her father as she possibly could. Lucian stood, still as a statue, eyes as glazed and unfocused as one of his zombie minions, while Dorabella scrambled to collect all the weapons safely at her side until the rest of the group would be able to retrieve them.

"It looks like Sator just removed Lucian from the equation," Eleonora commented. "At least for now, anyway."

"Now what?" questioned Isadora.

"Mommy!" Dorabella called from the other side of the cage.

"Just stay where you are!" Isadora yelled back. "I'll be there to get you in just a moment!"

"But how are we going to get out of here?" Felix said.

"Let's just see what the Higher Spirits do," Narena replied.

Sator and Arepo appeared to float as they made their way across the cavern to the make-shift cage. All it took was Sator slightly cocking his head, and the energetic barrier atop the stalagmites seemed to fall off and dissolve away. The Elder Triage was now able to leave the cage, but the group of little beings were still confined, unable to scale the stalagmites without the assistance of a taller being.

Seeing that there was no longer a blockage preventing them from leaving, the members of the Elder Triage reared their long, gangly legs over the stalagmites, stepping out over the bounds and standing, face to face, with Sator and Arepo. The Spirits studied each other for a brief moment, gazing to each Spirit with expressions of recognition. Then, suddenly, Magus lurched forward, his mouth opened in a silent scream that resembled an infinite black hole of nothingness. His arms reached for Sator's throat, but the deer's antlers swiped them away.

As the standoff of Higher and Under Spirits was occurring, Narena began to notice a slight humming in her ear, and as she paid more attention to it, noticed that if she really concentrated, she could make out words. Though wholly inaudible to her actual ears, the words seemed to resound within her head, and as she listened further, she determined that it was none other than the Higher and Under Spirits doing exactly what it was they were forbidden to do—speak.

Of course, since they were not speaking aloud, it would not have as negative of an impact as if it were in octaves that could be easily perceived by the living beings. But nevertheless, it *was* detectable, if only to Narena, a being who had experienced much in her lifetime with regards to the Spirits, and likely functioned at a higher vibration because of it.

Release the souls of the witches and wizard, Sator implored. *Possessing living beings will not get you to where you wish.*

Easy for you to say, Valerian within Magus replied. *You've reveled in keeping us at bay for generations, even in the most ancient of times.*

We are only trying to regain what we have lost over all this time, Doppel within Lorella added.

Yes, allow us to bring the ogres back to the Forest, and Gorgon will reign chaos no more, finished the other half of Doppel within Rhoslina, who had split himself to possess both Rhoslina and Lorella simultaneously. It was a feat only capable of an Under Spirit, though it was something that could not have provided much in the way of security for the Spirit within a living body. It was something likely suggested by the Controllers, and only possible with a difficult spell.

Your lust for more power than what you deserve is what only furthered the Forest's demise, Arepo said. *Lest you forget—if the Forest ceases to exist, so do we!*

We are merely following Gorgon's orders, Valerian replied. *Gorgon wants his ogres back, the Controllers know how to bring them back. This is the only way.*

And we are following the Yew's orders, Sator said. *The balance of light and dark, good and evil, is the only way that this Forest can exist. Without one, there cannot be the other, or else we would not know of either. The ogres would wreak havoc on the innocent and annihilate the land, which is why they were cast out in the first place. They cannot be allowed to return. We enacted a treaty with Gorgon for this very purpose, and now he has broken that treaty.*

Because of this, Arepo continued, *we have been given full permission to stop you in any way possible. We suggest you exit these bodies and take the Controllers back to the underworld with you. They were not approved for release.*

We no longer need your approval, Doppel within the witches said, causing a menacing echo when both women spoke at the same time in the same voice. *We've received it from the most powerful leader within the Forest. The Faery King broke that peace treaty when he aided in the release of the Controllers. There is no longer pure good within the Forest's kingdoms. All are corrupt, so now all will pay the price.*

Valerian within Magus suddenly turned to Narena, as if he were inherently aware that she was able to hear the Spirit conversation. He sneered, staring deeply into her soul, and spoke to Sator and Arepo, though keeping his lifeless, glowing yellow eyes on Narena.

Harmony doesn't live here anymore.

CHAPTER 21

Narena felt a chill run up her spine, but glared right back at the once-human that kept his menacing gaze locked on her. She then looked to Sator, who had helped her in the past during the time of the haunting, and suddenly was graced with what she thought was an excellent idea.

"Two of us need to let Sator and Arepo possess us!" she hissed. "It's the only way I can think of to fight Valerian and Doppel, short of performing two powerful spells like the ones Nessaba and King Alston did to stop the falling."

Myso exchanged glances with Basil, as did Felix with Eleonora. No one quite knew how to respond to that suggestion, though after what seemed like an eternity of silence, Myso finally spoke.

"And who do you suggest be the ones to be possessed?"

"I'll do it," Narena quickly offered. "Since it was my idea. But someone else has to volunteer."

"I'll be the other," Myso replied hurriedly.

"I actually think you two would be the best options, since you are both a lot more in tune with the Higher Spirits than the rest of us," Felix agreed.

"And while you two deal with the Elder Triage, the rest of us can go stop the Controllers," said Eleonora.

"That's a great idea," replied Narena. "And just so you are all in the know: the Controllers are performing a spell to release the ogres from captivity. Gorgon wants them back, and is using the Controllers to make that happen. Our friend," she said, nodding at Lucian, who was still frozen in place, "was indeed the one who released the Controllers. I'm guessing he was influenced by Gorgon to do that, though I don't know how."

"How do you know all of this?" Isadora asked.

"It sounds crazy, but I could hear the Spirits communicating with each other just now," Narena replied. "Like a distant hum of words, if that makes sense."

"It does to me!" Basil said. "At this point, it's really no explanation needed." The skunk chuckled, which seemed to momentarily lighten the mood.

"All right, now how do we go about getting the Higher Spirits to possess us?" Myso asked.

Narena thought for a moment, before saying, "Well, I suppose we'll need to get out of this enclosure first."

The group all exchanged glances with each other, before Narena finally offered a hopeful smile. "Being-ladder?" she suggested with a wink.

Felix laughed. "Great idea, Mother."

Basil walked over to the stalagmites that stood in the group's way, taking a brief survey of the height before crouching to the ground. "It'll likely take all of us to make this happen," he commented. "Okay, who's climbing up first?"

"I will," said Myso, pulling himself onto Basil's back. Felix went next, followed by Narena, Eleonora, and finally, Isadora. Once Isadora had made it to the top, she swung herself over the stalagmites, taking care not to get her clothes stuck on the pointed tips. She glanced quickly at the cave floor, mumbled a few incomprehensible words to herself, then allowed her body to drop. She landed on her feet. Dorabella ran over to her mother, and the two embraced, tears streaming down both of their faces. Then, Isadora looked back up.

"Toss me over," ordered Eleonora, prompting Narena to lift her arms upward in order to push Eleonora over the top. Eleonora followed her sister's lead, landing softly on her feet next to Isadora and her niece. Narena was tossed up next, followed by Felix, and finally Myso, who was aided by Basil standing on his back legs to give the troll the extra lift.

"But now what do I do?" asked the skunk, peering helplessly through the stalagmites and still enclosed within. The rest of the group eagerly received their weapons from Dorabella before scurrying to the edge of the doorway that led into the other cavern room.

But poor Basil didn't have a chance to be graced with a reply, as now the Under Spirit-possessed members of the Elder Triage began inching towards the now freed group of little beings. Sator and Arepo stepped forward as well, looking as though they meant to assist but not quite able to in their spirit forms. The Higher and Under Spirits were well-equipped to handle each other in their inherent states (much like how the Yew dealt with Labete-Agrimon during the falling), though when entered into a living-bodied being it would be a far simpler task to wage battle between other beings of flesh and blood.

Narena and Myso gave each other a quick glance before ducking around the looming witches and wizard, hurrying over to stand aside the two Higher Spirits. They made eye contact with Sator and Arepo, who nodded at them in reply.

"Sator," Narena whispered. "I give thee permission to enter my body. Use my abilities and my energy to enact a fair fight. Do so now, at this very moment—I command thee!"

Myso repeated Narena's words, though this time addressing Arepo. Instantly, the Higher Spirits' luminosity waned significantly, and they slowly began to disappear from view. Narena and Myso jolted simultaneously, and both could feel the sensation of the powerful entrance into their outward embodiments through the crown of their heads.

"Wow," Narena gushed. "So this is what it feels like."

Myso was not given an opportunity to comment on his own experience, as the members of the Elder Triage were now honing in on them completely, likely realizing that the Higher Spirits now resided within the two tiny beings.

Out of the corner of her eye, Narena noticed the rest of the group (minus Basil, who was still stuck in the enclosure and was now peering out from between two stalagmites) scurry out of the cavern room and back into the area where the Controllers were about to perform their spell. She turned her attention fully to the tall wizard who stood before her, taking in a quick gulp before drawing her blade from her boot, prompting Myso to follow suit.

"I don't want to kill you," she called upwards to the wizard. "I only want to remove the Under Spirit that possesses you. Please, allow me to perform an exorcism on you three!"

Magus let out a booming, unsettling laugh. "You think you can make me leave this body? Well, I have no intention of leaving. You'll have to destroy my body, which will kill these magical humans. Even then, my existence will live on. Make your choice, little one."

"Yes," Lorella rasped. "Kill or be killed, that is the new way of the Forest."

"We will do what we have to," Myso replied in a stoic manner.

"With the Higher Spirits within us, we should be able to exorcise the Under Spirits from them," Narena hissed to Myso. "I remember studying how this is done from one of the books in the palace library. I think I recall most of the words, and I'm just going to have faith that Sator and Arepo will provide the actual process. Hopefully we won't have to resort to violence to end this."

"I'll follow your lead," Myso whispered back. "Good luck, Narena. The Higher Spirits are with us."

Narena gave Myso a somber nod. She took a deep breath and exhaled, relaxing a bit upon feeling a tingle run up her spine and through the rest of her body. She turned to the Elder Triage, gazed into the eyes of Magus, and held up her hands, open-palmed. She began to speak, her voice sounding distant and not entirely her own.

"The Spirit inside has soiled your soul,
leave thy body now, you've taken your toll.
Release these beings from your adverse grasp,
by the power of the Higher Spirits—through them you now must pass!"

Magus grimaced briefly before releasing a guttural howl that reverberated against the walls of the cavern, as if Narena's words caused him internal physical pain. He swiped his hand across the ground, trying to knock Narena off of her feet, but just narrowly missed as she leaped out of the way at the very last second, prompting the wizard to swing his entire body around and come charging back at her, this time with more of a vigorous, daunting fervor.

Lorella and Rhoslina wasted no time coming furiously at Myso, their vocal chords gasping in a threatening sound. Their fingernails had grown long since the troll had last seen the witches, long enough, in fact, that they were able to be used as weapons. Myso discovered that the hard way, after Rhoslina gave him a good, crotchety-fingered swat across his face, resulting in a gash that sent a thick drop of warm, crimson blood trailing down his cheek. He was able to duck out of the way just in time to avoid a similar attack from Lorella.

Once Magus realized that he would not be able to catch little Narena, he began to focus upon the task of trying to stomp on her. His feet boomed onto the floor around her as she desperately tried to zig-zag around each impending step, pleading with Sator within her to help her however he could.

Narena's prayers were answered almost immediately, as she began to feel a surge of energy brewing underneath her skin.

"I trust you," she whispered to Sator, before enacting what she inherently felt was, at that exact moment, the right thing to do. She halted in her tracks, looking upwards at the wizard who loomed menacingly over her.

Magus lifted his enormous foot directly over Narena, licking his tongue across his lips as he perfected the location of his next, potentially fatal trample. Palms moist with sweat, Narena clasped her blade tightly in her hand, and waited for the inevitable stomp.

The wizard let out an echoing cackle and released his leg, stamping his booted foot down to the ground as hard as he possibly could. But just before he crushed little Narena into a pulp, the seasoned female nymph raised her blade high above her head, thrusting the point directly into the center of his foot. The sharpened blade pierced effortlessly through the bottom of Magus's worn-in boot, slicing through it and then deeply into the soft flesh of his foot. Before pulling her blade out with one swift movement, Narena managed to twist the blade, creating a rounded hole in the very center of the wizard's foot that seeped viscous blood so dark it looked like liquid obsidian. While Narena pulled back her blade and slipped out from under the foot, Magus wailed, pulling his leg back up and grabbing his wounded foot, hopping and flailing around as he continued to lose more and more of the thickened fluid. Narena quickly ran out of the way, crouching over by the enclosure as Basil reached a soft paw through and patted her shoulder comfortingly.

"Did Sator have you make a hole for Valerian to exit?" the skunk asked, to which Narena nodded silently, her eyes still fixated on the thrashing wizard. "Remember, Narena—once the Under Spirit is out, you must use Sator's energy to finish him!"

"This sounds familiar to me..." Narena trailed off for a moment before continuing, "If the Highest Spirit is not here to destroy the other, lesser Spirit, then the addition of a being of light will provide the extra oomph needed to fully vanquish the Spirit. Unless, of course, the Under Spirit is properly counterbalanced."

"Not just any being of light," Basil said. "A nymph is most favorable, remember?"

"I remember," Narena replied, glancing over at Myso, who was managing to keep Lorella and Rhoslina at bay for the time being.

Finally, Magus fell, his gigantic body crashing heavily upon the cavern floor. A pool of the darkened blood began to slowly form around his legs, tracing the outline of his fallen form. Suddenly, the likeness of a reebob started to emerge, pulling itself out from the hole at the bottom of

Magus's foot. First came the head, then the elongated, hairy arms, then a folded set of wings that spanned out immediately upon exiting the hole, followed by the legs and finally, the long, thin tail. The reebob hissed, then reared up to stand almost as tall as Magus himself.

"It's Valerian," Narena whispered. "He's out!"

"Now we need to get the two parts of Doppel out of Lorella and Rhoslina!" Myso called from afar, where he was now cornered by the two possessed witches.

"Just do what I did!" Narena shouted. "You need to puncture them and make a hole big enough for the Spirits to seep out!"

"I need your help!" Myso cried, helplessness apparent in his voice, which was quite uncommon for the troll.

"You have to hold them off until I can eliminate Valerian!" Narena called back.

But Valerian had other plans in mind, as he, in Spirit form, was soaring towards Rhoslina. In one swoop, the Spirit in likeness of a reebob slammed into her, shoving the second half of Doppel in his goblin likeness out through her agape mouth. The faded-looking Doppel seemed confused for a brief moment, then turned his attention to Lorella, who was watching with wide eyes and mouth agape. Doppel flew furiously into her open mouth, prompting the witch to jolt violently.

"Itching for a fair fight, huh?" Myso said to Lorella, who now had Valerian within her. "I wouldn't expect such from Under Spirits."

"There was a time when we thrived on the balance just the same as the Higher Spirits," Lorella replied menacingly. "But we were just waiting—biding our time until Gorgon would reign supreme, as he deserves." She grinned, her teeth far more rotten than Myso could ever recall.

"Looks like we both get one of them, now," Narena said, rushing over to the corner where Myso was now gazing up at both witches who loomed over him. Narena skidded to a halt next to the troll, having scooted past the witches' feet. "We need to puncture them. Try to make them step on you."

"Easier said than done," Myso griped, but held his blade at the ready anyway. "Be with me, Arepo," he muttered to himself as the witches closed further and further in. "Give me strength."

Lorella lurched forward, swiping her long, pointed fingernails at Myso as if trying to swat him like a bug. Luckily, Myso leaped out of the way, just barely avoiding being smacked into the rock-hard cave wall. Rhoslina lunged at Narena, trying to grab her, but Narena just narrowly missed being scooped up by the witch's hand. As Rhoslina whirled around by her wild swing, Narena jumped forward, stabbing her blade into the witch's ankle. She twisted the blade, though only standard-looking human blood spewed out, not the thick, darkened fluid that had drained from the bottom of Magus's foot.

"It has to be the bottom of their foot!" Narena yelled. "I don't know why!"

Lorella cackled. "In through the mouth, out through the foot," she sang mockingly, taking another swing at Myso, who swiped his blade right back at her. The metal cut across the center of Lorella's hand, causing her to slightly rear back as several drops of blood cascaded silently to the ground.

Words instantly popped into Myso's head, which he hurriedly repeated to Narena. "As above, so below." His eyes lit up, and his ears perked. "They must be released into the ground, or as close to the underworld as possible," he explained. "It *has* to be from the bottom of the foot!"

"If the Higher Spirits communicate through the crown of our heads during meditation," Narena added, slashing her blade to keep her distance from Rhoslina, "the Under Spirits would rule the bottom of our bodies—and the lowest part of the body is the bottom of the feet."

"How are we going to get them to lift a foot?"

"We have to trick them. Beat them at their own game."

"Okay then," Myso replied. "Are we ready?"

"Let's do this."

Myso moved forward, pretending to take a jab at Lorella's ankle. She smacked her hand down at him, attempting to squish his body into her leg. Myso suddenly felt a distinct tingling sensation scour through his body, and somehow intuitively knew that Arepo was gathering enough energy to assist him. Myso tried to think only thoughts to enhance the Higher Spirit's abilities to help him, as he knew it was very likely that the Controllers had been enacting powerful spells to gain the strength and energy that the Under Spirits would need. Myso knew that he would need to balance that with his own fervor in order to give Arepo what was needed to level the playing field.

As the intense tingling began to subside, Myso was graced with an idea, imparted into his mind from Arepo. He rushed to Lorella's shoes, which were pointed with black laces tied into a tight double knot. Using his blade, he sliced through the laces, making sure to leave parts of it long enough that it would provide a burden to Lorella's movements. As she bent down to fix her shoe, Myso swiped at her face, causing her to lean back to avoid the blow. The witch lost her balance, falling onto her rear end with a thud. Before she could pick herself up, Myso rushed in, piercing his blade into her now upturned foot. He twisted, and the blackened gooey blood instantly began pouring out as Lorella slammed to the ground.

"You have to get Rhoslina before Valerian fully emerges!" Myso cried.

Narena was already one step ahead of him, as she was already in the process of cutting through Rhoslina's shoelaces. The witch, having watched what had just occurred with Myso and Lorella, did not seem like she was going to bend down as readily as her sister had, so Narena knew that she needed to take a different approach.

As Rhoslina tried to kick at the little nymph, Narena saw an opening to rush over to the witch's ankle. Though this time, rather than taking the easy stab at it, Narena took the tips of her finger and began to lightly tickle the witch's leg, pivoting herself around it to cover the other side once the witch jolted in surprise. Narena kept tickling wherever she could around the witch's legs and ankles, providing just enough annoyance for Rhoslina to continue her attempts to rid herself of the nymph's harassment.

Finally, it seemed as though Rhoslina could take no more of the irritation. She lifted her leg to try to slap the tickling sensation away, giving Narena just enough time to swoop underneath her foot and thrust her blade upwards with a force she had never before possessed. The black, viscous bodily fluid seeped out, and Rhoslina fell heavily to the cave floor next to Lorella.

A thought popped into Narena's mind, so she wasted no time in speaking it aloud to Myso. "Now we need to give Sator and Arepo permission to leave our bodies so they can finish this," she said, to which Myso nodded in response. Both the nymph and troll closed their eyes, allowing Sator and Arepo to use just enough of their remaining energy to exit their bodies. A sensation began within their skulls, which quickly evolved into a throbbing pressure that caused the little beings to momentarily feel as though their heads might explode. But that feeling was short-lived, as both Myso and Narena began to notice that an almost blinding light radiated from the top of their heads, and as their thoughts of releasing the Spirits prevailed, Sator and Arepo slid from the crowns of their heads, making it look far more effortless than the process actually felt.

Freshly liberated from the living bodies, the four Spirits levitated, staring each other down. Sator and Arepo shined much brighter than Valerian and Doppel, who looked as though their forcibly enacted exit from the Elder Triage had taken a huge toll on their overall energy. Sator kicked his hoof and Arepo bobbed his head, as if signaling to each other to do what they must do to end this entire ordeal.

Sator and Arepo simultaneously shot themselves directly into the Under Spirits, fusing their Spirit forms into each other before molding all four into an amalgam of light and muddled darkness. As the four Spirits rolled further into one another, they began to slowly fade, vanishing into obscurity until nothing but the silent walls and empty cavern remained.

The Spirits were no more.

Chapter 22

Narena and Myso rushed over to Basil, gazing helplessly at the skunk still entrapped within the stalagmite enclosure.

"I don't know how we can get him out," Myso whined, his desperation to help his friend becoming more and more apparent.

"I wish I knew..." Narena trailed off, her eyes hurriedly looking for a solution.

"It's okay," Basil said. "You guys need to go help the others. I'll find a way out."

"Are you sure?" Narena asked. "It would be far better to have you with us to face the Controllers."

"Well, there's not much we can do right now," Basil replied. "Please—just go!"

Narena and Myso exchanged glances, until finally Myso sighed and gave a feeble shrug. "I guess our hands are tied on this one," he lamented.

"Okay, fine," Narena said. "But we'll be back for you—I promise!"

"Very well," Basil said. "Good luck!"

"Thank you," the two replied in unison, each grasping onto one of the skunk's paws and giving it a hopeful squeeze before turning to one another.

Then they left the cavern.

Narena and Myso crept into the other room of the mountain's cave, keeping as silent as they possibly could. As they turned the corner, they stopped, though they were both able to peek and see what was going on.

The Controllers had formed a circle around a bonfire that they had lit in the very center of the room, all dressed in their respective cloaks of red, blue, brown, and light gray. Within each Controller's hand was one of the realm crystals, with Celandine holding the fire, Bellis holding the water, Mullein holding the earth, and Elecampane holding the air. Their heads were lowered and their eyes closed, all mumbling the same incantation together. In the very corner, hidden behind the wall-shelf, the rest of the group of beings could be seen, carefully peering out and presumably waiting for the right opportunity to make a move. Almost instantly, Felix caught his mother's eye, and the two gave each other a nod, both sets of eyes wide in anticipation.

Celandine stepped forward, and began to speak more comprehensibly.

'For far too long you've been trapped, asleep.
You are no longer bound, it is your time to reap.
Awaken from your slumber, emerge from your binds,
Ogres of Gorgon—now is your time!'

Celandine reached into the pocket of her cloak and pulled out a velvet bag, pouring the contents into her open palm. It was the ash that she had used to control the zombies she'd created, and the Controller wasted no time in dipping her finger into the blackened dust and drawing a pattern that formed around the coven's circle.

"Oh, no," Narena whispered. "We're too late!"

"There is still hope," Myso hissed. "The spell is not yet complete. Watch!"

The Controllers all reached into the pockets of their cloaks, pulling out an item that represented their element: a lava rock, a piece of coral, a moss-covered stone, and an eagle's feather. They placed their items around the fire in a circle, before Mullein headed over to the shelf area where the rest of the group was hiding. They ducked back behind the make-shift shelf as he approached, though luckily he did not seem to notice them. He grabbed a large wooden box and shook it around, prompting the sound of muffled wails to resonate through the cave. Something living was within that box, and whatever it was, it was not happy to be in there.

Narena's heart sank as Mullein opened the box, making his way back to rejoin his siblings. He pulled out four small creatures: a sparrow, a glass jar that contained a fish, a field mouse, and finally, a salamander. It took all of Narena's efforts not to rush into the room and attempt to save the poor, helpless creatures, but Myso sensed her escalating emotional response and held tightly onto her shoulders from behind, giving her a sympathetic squeeze.

"They're not going to..." Narena gulped, "sacrifice them, right?"

"I'm afraid that's what it looks like," Myso replied. "But I truly hope that I am wrong."

"Me, too," Narena squeaked.

Mullein calmly walked around the circle, handing each elemental creature to the element that they represented. The Controllers repositioned themselves as they were before, and put their hoods over their heads, bowing them once more.

Then, far too effortlessly, they each took turns tossing the innocent creatures into the fire, which seemed to ominously moan on its own as each poor individual was tossed within it. Narena started to scream, but Myso quickly slapped his hand over her mouth, suppressing her uncontrollable cries.

"I'm so sorry," was all the troll whispered, as he felt the wetness of Narena's tears gently roll down the back of his hand. "Please, Narena, there's nothing more we can do for them."

"Except avenge their souls," Narena hissed. "And I have every intention of doing so."

"Save that energy," Myso replied. "You're going to need it soon."

The Controllers began to murmur incomprehensibly once again, focusing their words downwards, towards the underworld. At this point, only the word "Gorgon" could be heard, repeated over and over again as the coven of siblings called his power to aid in their spell. They were likely unaware that the rest of the Under Spirits were no more, but as it seemed that sentiment would have had little effect on the outcome of their spell regardless.

The fire expanded, roaring upwards towards the ceiling of the cavern and billowing thick, black smoke that trailed out through the entrance of the cave. The Controllers then each placed their crystals, along with their realm items, around the circle to create four distinct points. They grasped onto each others' hands, held their arms up high, and bowed their entire torsos almost entirely to the ground. Then they released their hands, and looked to one another, smiling.

"It is almost complete," Celandine beamed, her eyes sparkling. "Now all we must do is wait for the sign."

Felix's impulsiveness must have gotten the better of him, as he suddenly came charging out from behind the wall shelf, swinging his blade through the air with Eleonora following closely behind. Isadora and Dorabella stayed behind, but Narena and Myso took the cue from their king to come rushing out from their hiding place as well.

The Controllers, understandably surprised by the presence of the beings that they assumed had been taken care of by the possessed Elder Triage, drew their attention to the little ones that were now rapidly approaching them. Felix scrambled around Elecampane's legs, managing to swipe his blade across his ankle, while Eleonora was able to cut across the back of Bellis's calf. Narena and Myso arrived with just enough time to provide powerful swipes of their blades onto the Achilles tendons of Celandine and Mullein, retreating out of the way just in time to avoid the forceful stomps of the Controllers' feet that inevitably resulted from their attack.

"You think you can stop us?" Celandine laughed, rubbing her hand across her tendon and peering curiously at the coagulated blood that stained her fingers. "I'm afraid you're too late."

"But it's okay," Bellis continued with an eerie grin. "It will be far better for you to perish by our hands than by those of the ogres. I'm sure your souls will thank us for that."

"They won't be provided that opportunity, I'm afraid," a bellowing voice called from behind.

All heads turned to witness a very exhausted-looking Magus in the doorway to the cavern where the Spirit battle had recently been waged, with Lorella and Rhoslina standing to either side of the wizard. Behind them, Basil stood, presumably released from the enclosure by the much larger humans.

Celandine cackled, the sound echoing through the chamber. "You're too late," she repeated, her mouth curling upwards in her trademark unsettling smile. "No one—not even the Elder Triage, not even the Higher Spirits—can help you now."

"That's where you're wrong!" Felix shouted. "You are outnumbered now. Just surrender and you will be sent back to your realms where you belong!"

"Those realms are no longer our homes," Mullein replied calmly. "This Forest is, and it will be—for the rest of eternity."

"If you will not go willingly," Felix replied boldly, "then we will forcibly send you to the underworld!"

"By killing us?" Elecampane mocked. "Oh, no! Please, little Nymph King... Don't send us to the big, bad underworld!"

Felix felt his face grow exceedingly hot as his anger boiled at the siblings' dismissal of his words. His thoughts spoke volumes within his mind, and yet they were so muddled that he couldn't, for the life of him, form any sequence of words that would further intimidate his foes. So he said nothing, and instead furiously glanced over at Magus, whose hand was lifted, holding something shiny.

"Looking for this?" Magus asked, revealing a pure white, iridescent crystal peppered with gold in his palm. "I'm sure you need it, as it is undoubtedly the most powerful crystal of them all."

"What does he have there?!" Mullein shouted. "That's not what I think it is, right, Celandine? How could they possibly have obtained it?"

Celandine calmly grinned, chuckling as she slowly inched closer to Magus and further away from the circle. "It *must* be the Spirit crystal," she said. "How this wizard has it is beyond me. But either way, I don't intend to allow him to hold it with his weak, grubby hands for long."

Celandine rushed at Magus, shrieking in fury as she rapidly approached. She tackled the elderly wizard to the ground, slashing her long fingernails at his face. In their scuffle, the crystal flew out of Magus's hand, bouncing several times along the cave floor before coming to a stop just in front of Elecampane's feet.

"Ah," Elecampane said, picking it up. "How serendipitous."

Before he could mock the little group of beings any further, Felix fired an arrow at the Controller that pierced his wrist directly through his crescent moon tattoo, the obsidian tip emerging at an angle through the top of his hand. He wailed, dropping the crystal to the ground once more, which rolled over to the make-shift shelf where Isadora and Dorabella were still hiding.

Dorabella popped out, rushing over to the crystal and picking it up before darting back into the crevice behind the shelf just as Mullein dove to the ground, his arms desperately reaching for the crystal.

"Give it to me, you wretched brat!" he yelled, extending his arm as far back into the crevice as he could. Blind to where his hand was searching, he patted around in all directions as Isadora and Dorabella tried desperately to squeeze their bodies as far back as possible. Isadora shoved her daughter behind her, but in doing so provided Mullein's hand with just the right opportunity to grasp tightly onto her leg, dragging the faery out into the open and tossing her to Bellis like a rag doll.

"Give us the crystal or watch your mother die!" Celandine shrieked, her anger becoming more and more apparent in the tone of her voice. "You have until the count of three to hand over that Spirit crystal or else we will kill her! *One... two...*"

Dorabella rummaged into her pocket, pulling out the amethyst that she had taken from their earlier quest in Gnome Kingdom. Muttering a quick incantation of illusion that she'd learned from an old book she'd once read, the faery child cupped her hands tightly around the crystal, infusing her energy into the gem in order to further enhance the spell. She located Mullein's calloused hand in the darkness and placed the crystal within it before safely securing the Spirit crystal in her pocket. Mullein's hand retreated, and Dorabella started to creep out of her hiding place.

Once her eyes adjusted to the dim lighting of the cave, Dorabella hurried over to her mother, who had wriggled out of Bellis's grasp and been dropped onto the ground. The two faeries ran over to Felix and Eleonora, and Dorabella slyly slipped the Spirit crystal into her uncle's pocket. Felix gave his niece a slight wink, then shot an arrow at Bellis, slicing into her left ear cartilage and giving her the appearance of wearing a quite fashionable arrow earring. Bellis wailed, looking to her sister for assistance, but as it seemed Celandine was already one step ahead of her.

"Let's eliminate these pesky crystals once and for all, shall we?" Celandine said, motioning for her siblings to join her in picking up the realm crystals from the circle. They gazed at one another, and with gruesome grins, tossed all five crystals into the depths of the fire.

The fire gulped as if it had just eaten a hearty meal, then shot up, sparking every which way and billowing even denser smoke than it had before.

"You're welcome to come retrieve what's left of those crystals now," Celandine mocked. "This enchanted fire of Gorgon can consume anything—even that which is not meant to be burned." She turned to her siblings, then to the group of beings, and offered a haughty, self-indulgent smirk.

"Let's see you try to stop us now."

CHAPTER 23

h, Celandine?" Felix called, a twinkle of mischief dancing in his eyes.

"What?!" she cried, her irritation still readily apparent.

"Did you mean to dispose of this?"

Felix held the Spirit crystal in the palm of his hand, the paleness of his skin illuminated with a radiance that seemed to emanate from within. The crystal was charged with energy, an energy that only could have come from the Higher Spirits, possibly a gift in exchange for their sacrifice.

As if on cue, the Elder Triage bowed their heads in unison, and began chanting an incantation:

"Your time has ended, your reign is through,
the reckoning will provide to you what is due."

Myso and Narena joined in the chant and focused their minds as well, gaining energy to help implement the Elders' spell. Dorabella was also honing in to that energy, as was Isadora, Eleonora, and of course,

Felix. As the incantation intensified, the crystal shone more and more brightly. Suddenly, the entire cave began to shake violently, the ground shifting back and forth and the walls vibrating so intensely that it was hard to maintain balance for everyone in question.

"It's the sign from Gorgon!" Celandine exclaimed with glee. "The spell worked!"

"No, it didn't!" shouted Felix as forcefully as he could. "You have merely underestimated the magical power of the Elder Triage!"

"Poppycock!" Celandine cackled. "Their magic is no match for us!"

"Um, Celandine?" Elecampane asked, his voice uncharacteristically nervous.

Celadine's eyes frantically darted around, her expression befuddled. "What?" she repeated.

"Something's happening... My feet are getting all tingly..."

Sure enough, Elecampane's existence was waning, in a manner unconcerned with time and space. It moved up his legs, up his torso, and finally, overtook his neck.

"Oh, no..." he said, as his face shook in visibility, until finally his entire being was absorbed into thin air.

Celandine turned to Bellis, who had begun to scream in agonizing frustration. Water was raging up her legs, swirling in a hurricane of furious mist. As the level rose, Bellis's wails became more helpless, until her head was fully submerged. Her eyes wide in terror, the water consumed itself, engulfing Bellis until she, too, was no more.

Mullein reached for Celandine's hand, just as a rumbling began that nearly knocked everyone off of their feet. The earth shook, shooting a formation of stalagmites that resembled a human hand up from the ground, trapping Mullein within their grasp. He grunted, trying desperately to climb out, but before he could, a hole emerged from the ground, and Mullein was only given a split second to gaze feebly into his sister's fiery eyes before he was swallowed by the earth.

Celandine stood before the group of little beings, seemingly admitting defeat in her stance and demeanor. She held her arms out wide, accepting her impending, inevitable fate. The ground beneath her feet grew maliciously hot, and as the fire surged up the length of her body, she looked one last time into the eyes of Eleonora, who had not been able to look away from the Controllers' demises.

"I never should have let you go..." was all Celandine said to the Nymph Queen, her very last words before the fire coiled entirely around her face, charring it black as the ash she used for her spells. Her piercing eyes still glowed brightly, striking into Eleonora until the woman was completely swallowed by the fire. Celandine's eyes were the last to remain, slowly fading away moments after her body had disappeared.

"Esmeralda..." faintly echoed through the walls of the cave until there was nothing left of the Controllers' former existences, leaving only an eerie silence in their wake.

Back in Nymph Kingdom, Kellen had been resting in his bed, missing his wife while dreamily shifting his gaze from the window to his casted leg, propped up to quicken the healing process. When Druzy flew hurriedly into the room, buzzing in circles around the nymph's head, Kellen barely even noticed. It wasn't until Druzy spoke—well, screamed at him, rather— that Kellen's attention was drawn to the frenzied insect.

"Kellen? Sir? Please, I have some troubling news..."

Kellen snapped to attention, as if still in his warrior days, the time he considered to be his prime. "Yes?"

"Sir, I know you are limited in your ability to move, however please do not let the news I am about to impart upon you injure you further..."

"Please, Druzy," Kellen said. "The message?"

"Yes, um, well... I'm afraid your father, Felide, has passed away. He slipped out of the palace last night and ventured out into the Forest. Apparently, he was willing and ready for his soul to move on. He left a note..."

Druzy dropped a balled-up piece of parchment onto Kellen's lap. The nymph uncurled the letter and read it silently to himself.

My dearest son Kellen,

My love for you knows no bounds, though I admit there were times when my desire for respect outweighed showing you that love. I pray that I was not too hard on you. I hope that I have taught you strength, as it is the virtue that I was forced to learn on my own. I know deep within my heart that now is my time. I look forward to seeing your mother, and eventually meeting you again in my next lifetime. I love you. Please never forget that.

Until next time,

Father

Kellen felt the tears begin to well in the back of his eyes, but could not allow them to come forward.

"Very good," was all he said, before delicately folding his father's note and sliding it into his breast pocket.

"I am very sorry, sir," Druzy said.

"It is quite all right," Kellen replied.

"Would you like to be alone?"

Kellen thought for a moment, before taking in a long breath. "No," he said. "This time, I'd actually prefer the company."

CHAPTER 24

"Are they gone from our Forest?" Dorabella's small, soft voice was the first to reverberate through the cavern once all the Controllers had disappeared.

"Yes, my child," Myso replied quietly. "They've either been sent back to their realms, or they've perished. Which one it was, however, I do not know."

"Either way, they will not be returning to our Forest," Narena assured. "Even if they survived the power of the Spirit crystal, it will take them many generations before they'd be able to muster enough energy to return. At least, I hope."

"What should we do about the Spirit crystal?" Eleonora inquired. "Where would be the best place to keep it?"

"Keep it at Nymph Palace," Magus replied. "I think the nymphs have proven that they are among the most formidable opponents in the Forest. I have faith that it will be the most protected with you, Felix."

Felix smiled. "I will ensure that it is heavily guarded at all times. You have my word."

"After all I've been through with the nymphs," Magus began. "I'd say that a nymph's word is as good as a wizard's! Well, almost." He gave Felix and Eleonora a wink.

"But what about Lucian?" Isadora broke in. "He remains still as a stone. Not that I'm complaining."

"There is no longer space for life to dwell within him," Magus broke in, his tone sounding like it was still weakened. "He is dead."

"Serves him right," Felix said. "He aided in the release of the Controllers, which caused the reckoning. Therefore, it is only fair that he should die with it." He looked at Dorabella, and his demeanor softened a bit. "Though his powerful blood will live on, in a much better being than he ever was."

"Nice save, sweetheart," Eleonora teased, drawing the Nymph King's attention to her. Felix embraced his wife, gently laying a soft kiss on her cheek. Eleonora leaned in to her husband's face, her lips just above his ear. She let out a sigh, then calmly whispered, "I'm pregnant."

Felix's eyes widened with excitement. "You are?! How do you know?"

"I can just feel her. The soul entered just before we faced the Controllers."

"Her?!"

"My intuition has heightened to an almost terrifying degree," Eleonora joked.

"I wasn't going to say anything," Narena broke in. "But I had a feeling..."

"Yeah, you started acting like a pregnant being days ago," chimed in Isadora, who was smiling more brightly than anyone (except perhaps Dorabella and Eleonora) had ever seen her. She embraced her sister, unable to hold back her tears of happiness. "Did you hear that, Dora?

You're getting a baby cousin!"

Isadora turned back to her once-faery sister, unable to fully express just how truly ecstatic she was for her. Perhaps it was the combined emotions of their harrowing journey and battle, or the realization of the importance of sisterhood, and the love that existed within sisters' hearts whether it was always apparent or not. But for whatever reason, and whether or not they were aware of it, Isadora and Eleonora made a subconscious agreement in that very moment to focus on cherishing that love and embracing their differences, but also celebrating and appreciating the many attributes they were proud to share. The respect that they had gained for one another during their recent experiences was just what was needed to solidify the sanctity of their relationship, never again providing even the slightest need to shake that strong foundation. Life was too precious, too important.

All the members of the group gathered together, embracing and allowing their tears of joy to flow freely. When they had finally finished their celebration, they gathered themselves and prepared to leave, properly dressing any wounds they had received during their recent battle. When all were ready, they left the cave and bid goodbyes before going their separate ways, with Magus, Lorella, and Rhoslina headed back to their house. The rest of the group accepted the kind offer from Emerson and Shelley to be flown back to Nymph Kingdom, and once they arrived the two crows bid everyone their goodbyes, as it was time for the birds to begin their yearly nesting routine, a welcomed normalcy after all their tribulations.

Despite the luxurious means of their travel home, it was still quite a long journey even by air, so by the time the group arrived, all were exhausted and ready to sleep for as long as they possibly could. Upon their arrival, however, the group was greeted by Druzy, who sadly informed them of Felide's passing.

Felix immediately rushed to Kellen's bedside, saying nothing as he approached, arms opened wide to embrace his father.

"Thank you, my son," Kellen whispered as Narena and Eleonora entered the room and sat on the foot of the bed. "I'm afraid it was his time."

"I have a feeling Grandfather was not afraid," was all Felix replied.

"There is hope," Narena offered softly. "My darling, Eleonora is pregnant."

Kellen's eyes instantly lit up, glistening with excitement that danced madly through his voice. "I'm going to be a grandpa?!"

The family embraced, a sense of peace and stillness blanketed around them, something they had not felt in a long time. Hope was indeed, not lost. In fact, it was only growing stronger.

Chapter 25

In Faery Kingdom, news of Lucian's demise spread quickly. The royals and members of the court were devastated, as the plans for an uprising of power within the faeries was now no longer an option. The normal, everyday faeries, however, were pleased to hear that Lucian had perished, and once the entire kingdom became aware of the empty throne, protests broke out, surrounding the palace with the shouts and wails of hundreds of fed-up faeries.

"We demand a fair king!" shouted the disturbed citizens. "We want a king who adequately represents our kind!"

True, the conspiracy amongst the faery royals and the Controllers had promised the faeries a better life—more resources, less visitors, and a stronger voice in the affairs of all the surrounding kingdoms. While the idea had sounded appealing to the people at the beginning, when they'd learned what it would truly entail, most faeries changed their stance on their kingdom's increase in power. Now, it seemed, the faeries longed for the balance that many of their kind had gone to great lengths to try to upend. Perhaps the faeries' sensitive natures made them more susceptible to the negative influence that had begun to spread during the time of the falling, and as more eyes opened to the effects of the reckoning, they began to awaken to the truth.

After many days of relentless protesting, members of the court finally emerged from their barricade within the palace, onto a balcony where they could address the ever-growing crowd directly. The imbalance in the energy of the Forest had caused those with power to be entirely consumed by it, resulting in a weariness to accept the changes that were inevitably needed to keep the kingdoms in harmony. Finally, it was decreed that an election would soon take place, and since there were no known heirs to the throne (that the court was aware of, anyway), regular faery citizens were encouraged to submit their interest to earn the right to campaign for the position. Few stepped forward, as many worried for the safety of their families and loved ones, though after several days the court declared to the faeries that they had narrowed the selection down to two.

As the time of reckoning in the Forest slowly but surely began to transition into a time of heightened awareness, the kingdoms started to gradually shift into more peaceful times. The Forest was becoming more balanced, as the Higher and Under Spirits had been diminished to only the Yew and Gorgon. But despite the equity of light and dark, the negativity that had loomed in the Forest for far too long was not ready to give up its reign. Though the inhabitants of the kingdoms were prepared to move into a time of awakening, the ability to completely renew the Forest would require them to first address the negativity that remained, before a true awakening could even begin to occur.

Far, far away, in a land not explored by any being who dwelt within the Forest, a mountain stood triumphantly high, tall enough that it was able to peer down at Lapis Mountain with ease, even at the great distance that it stood from the Forest's peak. Within this mountain, gargantuan creatures began to emerge, shaken out of an enchanted torpor that kept them confined for a time unbeknownst to the awareness of their souls. They were somewhat misshapen in appearance, as though whomever had sculpted their existences had either given up mid-process or intended for them to look as unsettling and gruesome as they did. Slightly hunched, with arms much longer than their legs, the entire remaining population of ogres marched forth from their captivity in utter determination.

The ogres stomped through their land, providing no consideration to the ground they walked upon, and giving absolutely no regard to any living being or creature that stood in their way. They would need to feast, train for the tasks ahead, and carefully plan their reinstatement to the place where they had long been forbidden to ever return.

Once they were fully ready, vengeance would be served, but until then...

They would wait.

About the Author

T. Damon has always harbored an immense passion for not only writing, but animals and nature. Her added interest in all things magical and mythical inspired the creation of The Forest Spirit series, which embodies a little bit of everything she loves. When she's not writing, she enjoys spending time with her husband, daughter, and pets at her home in the enchanted forests of Northern California.

Other Works by the Author

Writing *As* T. Damon

The Falling: Book 1 of The Forest Spirit series

The Haunting: Book 2 of The Forest Spirit series

The Awakening: Book 4 of The Forest Spirit series
(Coming soon!)

Perchance to Dream:
"The Desperate Warrior and the Beast Who Walks Without Sound"
(Also available as a stand-alone paperback)

Writing *As* K.L. Teal

A Girl Named Dracula

Anthropoidea